the CHEROKEE STRIP

THE BRANDIRON SERIES

the CHEROKEE STRIP

BOOK TWO

DUSTY RICHARDS

THREE-TIME SPUR AWARD WINNER

with DENNIS DOTY

GALWAY PRESS

an imprint of
THE OGHMA PRESS

OGHMA
CREATIVE MEDIA

Bentonville, Arkansas • Los Angeles, California
www.oghmacreative.com

Library of Congress Cataloging-in-Publication Data

Names: Richards, Dusty, author.
Title: The Cherokee Strip/Dusty Richards. | The Brandiron #2
Description: Second Edition. | Bentonville: Galway, 2021.
Identifiers: LCCN: 2021934062 | ISBN: 978-1-63373-558-3 (hardcover) |
ISBN: 978-1-63373-559-0 (trade paperback) | ISBN: 978-1-63373-195-0 (eBook)
Subjects: BISAC: FICTION/Westerns | FICTION/Action & Adventure |
FICTION/Historical/General
LC record available at: https://lccn.loc.gov/2021934062

Galway Press hardcover edition March, 2021

Jacket & Interior Design by Casey W. Cowan
Editing by Gordon Bonnet & Amy Cowan

Published by Galway Press, an imprint of The Oghma Press, a subsidiary of The Oghma Book Group.

This one's for Gil

FOREWORD

MY GRANDFATHER, LLOYD, WAS of what was probably the last generation of the original cowboy. Born in Indian Territory, he grew up near Roswell, New Mexico, and one of his first jobs was as a wrangler on what was once John Chisum's Jinglebob Ranch. He was a great storyteller, and as a result, I grew up with a love of the west and anything cowboy.

I had been writing short stories for maybe a dozen years and even an unpublished Western novel, when I submitted a story to *Saddlebag Dispatches* in early 2017. I expected to wait the usual two or three months for either an acceptance or a rejection. Much to my surprise, just a couple days later, I received a telephone call from the co-founder of Oghma Creative Media, Casey Cowan, who at that time was the Publisher of *Saddlebag Dispatches* as well as the parent organization.

He said that he'd read my story and shared it with Dusty Richards, the much beloved and award-winning western author. I learned that Dusty had not only read my story, but also my bio which mentioned that I was a free-lance copy editor. Dusty told Casey, "We need to sign this guy as a writer and an editor." It would be an understatement to say that I was shocked. I had only recently added editor to my resume and, at the time, had only four or five paying clients.

After some thought, and a discussion with my wife, I accepted. By early fall of that year, I had turned in my first assigned novel edit, and Dusty asked that I be assigned to edit his books. A telephone call was scheduled so that Dusty and I could discuss his forthcoming unpublished works and form a plan to edit and release them. Unfortunately, before we could begin working together, both Dusty and his wife, Pat, were taken from us in a tragic auto accident. The world of western writers had lost a giant much too soon.

Honoring Dusty's wishes, I've gone on to edit seven of his novels and two short story collections. Along the way, I've become the curator of the Dusty Richards collection at Oghma and the Publisher of Dusty's brainchild magazine, *Saddlebag Dispatches.*

Although he missed the era of the Pulp Western which jump-started many legendary western writers, Dusty still managed to write and publish as many novels as most of the legends he loved. He was able to find that in-spiration in nearly everything and fashion an immersive story from it. With over 150 published works, he still left a box full of notes and ideas he never had time to finish.

One of Dusty's trademark characteristics was his version of the Cowboy Code. He was never too busy or too famous to help another writer along the way, and the world of Western Fiction is better for it. Several of the western writers I've published in *Saddlebag Dispatches* got a leg up, an encouraging word, or good advice from Dusty in their own journeys.

The Cherokee Strip is a typical Dusty Richards creation, a masterful mix of the landscapes and realism of L'Amour and the bigger than life colorful characters of Johnstone and Brand. Like L'Amour, Dusty wrote of places and regions he was familiar with, and he was just as big and colorful as any of his characters.

He knew the land and the people that form the backdrop to his stories, and more importantly, he genuinely loved them.

Dusty was at home wherever he happened to be. From the announcer's booth or sitting his horse while announcing a rodeo, at the speaker's podium at a conference or awards dinner, or simply having a meal with friends at some Arkansas diner, Dusty was just Dusty. He wasn't one to put on airs or let his head outgrow his trademark hat.

The Cherokee Strip is a story or ordinary people doing extraordinary things much like the real world of cattle drives, town-taming marshals, and Indian fighters his stories represent. Dusty knew the world he wrote of and would have been perfectly at home and immensely successful in it. Tough cowboys, trail herds, outlaws, and painted women make this yet another Dusty page turner.

At the request of Dusty's family and publisher, I've been honored to take on the task of completing some of his unfinished projects, expanding others which were too short, and collecting more of his short stories. This has been an immense challenge. *The Cherokee Strip* is one of those stories.

Like most authors, Dusty had his own unique voice and staying true to that voice while adding additional material or writing original stories from his notes in the way I believe Dusty would have told them is incredibly difficult. I've certainly tried my best, but Dusty's many fans and readers will be the final judge of my success. I pray that the reader will not be able to distinguish which parts of *The Cherokee Strip* are Dusty's and which are my own.

I hope you enjoy it.

—Dennis Doty
Corbin, Kentucky
January 12, 2021

THE BRANDIRON SERIES

the CHEROKEE STRIP

CHAPTER No. 1

NORMAN THOMPSON TRIED to mind his own business, but sometimes business finds you.

He'd left Montana that spring after getting into a gunfight—one of those things that starts out with a few hot words in a saloon and escalates so quickly you don't know what hit you. It'd been over a horse. Always seemed like it was over a horse or a woman. But this time, it was an ugly-looking pair of brothers who claimed that Norm had sold them a stallion with a bum leg. Norm suspected the injury had happened after the sale, and the men were trying to get him to take back a lame animal, and he told them so.

Ten minutes later one of the brothers was dead and the other bleeding from a bullet graze to the shoulder. Norm was unharmed, but the injured man fixed him with an evil stare and said, "I'll see you dead for this, Thompson," and ran out of the saloon leaving the door swinging so hard it about flew off the hinges.

Seemed like a good enough time to get out and find another venue.

There are times you can't avoid trouble however hard you try. All summer he'd drifted around western Nebraska looking for work as a ranch foreman without any luck. What he came across instead was a serious fistfight with a total stranger. In an alley beside the Elk Saloon in Ogallala, he ran into a guy who was slapping his wife around. He stepped in and separated them.

"I don't know who the hell you are, mister, but you better get the hell out of here," the woman-beater said to Norm, red-faced with rage. He wasn't that big a guy, but he was no small weakling either. They were soon circling each other, their fists raised, mad as two angry alley cats ready to tangle.

"Mister, where I come from, real men don't slap around women." With Norm's attention centered on his opponent, he wondered if this man had any backup that he needed to note.

"Why don't you mind your own damn business? That bitch is mine, and I'll slap her all I want."

Circling the abuser, Norm saw that their argument had drawn a crowd. His heart wasn't into having a big city brawl with this guy. His intention had been to simply make him agree to stop abusing her. But obviously, his adversary was a real bully and wanted to show off. They'd sure become the point of a crowd's interest in a short time. Next thing, the law would be down there and lock both of them up for fist fighting in public.

Norm dropped his right shoulder, and, when the man came at him swinging again, he found a perfect opening and connected with a powerful uppercut to his chin. The blow lifted the man right off his boot heels.

At least the fight had ended quickly. He looked down at the man, lying on his back in the dust. He massaged his knuckles. Damn, his right hand sure felt sore from hitting him that hard.

"That's Jake Elder," an onlooker said pointing at the victim on the ground. "There's a five hundred dollar reward from Wells Fargo on him."

Norm looked at the crying young woman holding her face and leaning on the siding of the Elk Saloon. "Is he really Jake Elder?"

She nodded.

"What's going on here?" an officer in a black derby hat demanded.

"Sir, I have just apprehended a big-name outlaw."

"Who is he?"

"Jake Elder."

"By God, it might be him. Who told you it was him?"

"That young lady that he was slapping around back here."

The marshal looked around, then frowned at him. "What young lady are you talking about?"

A real crowd had gathered by then, and somehow, she must have slipped away. Damn it, why did she do that? He hadn't even officially met her. The officer, however, had already lost interest. He disarmed the still groggy outlaw and jerked him to his feet.

"You're going to jail, Elder." The officer handcuffed his hands behind his back then started him in that direction.

The man spoke for the first time since the fight. His voice was surly. "I ain't Elder."

"With all the crimes you've been charged with, I wouldn't be him either." The lawman turned to Norm. "What's your name?"

"Norman Thompson."

"You better come along, too, and fill out the papers on his capture. Wells Fargo ain't like most of those outfits. They pay their rewards pretty fast. This may be your lucky day in Ogallala. Everyone clear out of here. This fight is all over."

Norm followed along behind the officer and his captive, but the entire walk to the jail his mind kept going back to wondering where she'd gone off to. It bothered him that she might need some money or care. No telling. She wasn't his ward, that was for sure, but he'd like to help her out if she was in real need. His quick vision of her, long light brown hair hanging in her face, cheeks wet with tears—he still thought under it all was a real pretty lady. Was she Elder's wife? Concubine? No telling about a female who was attached to a wanted outlaw.

The desk officer at the jail recognized Elder when they came in the door and asked how Marshal McQuire had apprehended him.

"This man here, Norman Thompson, did it with his bare hands in the alley beside the Elk Saloon."

The desk officer grinned. "Wow, I won't mess with you, mister. Why, he's one of the most wanted outlaws in Nebraska."

Norm simply nodded and thanked the man like it was nothing, and he did that sort of thing every day.

But the officer wasn't done yet. He laughed. "Mister, when the news gets out they may have a parade for you and a big ol' banquet."

"I just want to fill out the papers, collect the reward, then get on with my business." He had no big hero celebration plans for himself. It was all pure-dee luck he fell into his capture anyway.

But he saw right off the desk officer was not going to let him off so easy. He was as eager as a puppy. "Being a bounty hunter, do you get in some real messes being by yourself?"

"No."

He whistled. "Damn, you're a tough guy."

"Mister?" Norm said.

"O'Brian's me name."

"Officer O'Brian, I usually work on ranches as a hand or a boss. I came up here from Texas with a big herd of cattle, and I'm looking for some ranch work."

"Neat undercover position for a bounty man. Who'd think some cowboy was really rounding up criminals? Bet you fooled Elder all to pieces. When did you know you had him?"

"After I knocked him on his ass."

"He never went for his gun?"

"No, I'd'a shot him."

"Fast draw huh? The reward said dead or alive. Paid the same amount. Shake my hand, I have heard all about bounty men like you. But I never met a true bounty hunter until right now."

He shook the man's hand feeling a little foolish about the whole matter. He filled out the papers to collect his reward and gave them to the deskman while they strip-searched Elder. The outlaw made a big noise while being herded off to his cell in his underwear.

He shook a fist. "If we ever meet again, I damn sure promise to kill you."

Norm shrugged, which made the outlaw madder, and he ended with a stream of foul language as the cell door clanged shut behind him.

"I wouldn't worry about him, Mister Thompson," Officer O'Brian said. "By the time he's out of there, you'll have cashed the reward check and be long gone from these parts, if that's what you want."

"How long before they pay this money?"

"Oh, less than two weeks."

"I'll be around town. I get a job, and I'll leave word where I am going to be."

O'Brian laughed out loud. "Going undercover again. Smart move."

"Thank the other marshal, too." He left the jail and went back to the area of the Elk Saloon to try and find the woman that Elder had been beating up on.

He ordered a beer. The bartender poured the drink and put it in front of him on the dusty bar, then leaned over and said under his breath, "I figured that son of a bitch was wanted when he first started to hang around here."

"Where did she go?"

"That woman? She's right out the back door working in the tent with the star on it. Highest priced hooker in the alley."

He set the beer down. "What's her name?"

"Kathy Starr."

For a long moment he stared at the foam on the beer. Wow, he didn't expect that. But he knew that, if she was connected to outlaws, she wasn't singing in the Methodist Church Choir either. "Thanks."

What a helluva morning this had turned out to be. He started out taking the side of what he thought was some innocent girl being beat up by her bully of a mate. Instead she turned out to be the number one entertainer among the tenthouse prostitutes.

Norm was no more a purveyor of shady ladies than he was a bounty hunter, but he still felt she might need some help. Maybe it was dumb, but he'd always felt about such women that there had to be some weakness behind their tough, hard-edged professional front. She had to have some softer feelings like his sisters and mother possessed.

Norm finished his beer then made up his mind to go talk to her. He paid the bartender a dime and went straight out the back door into the bright sunshine.

The front flap was down on the wall tent bearing the painted white star on both sides of the roof. Standing before the flap he cleared his throat. "Ma'am are you home?"

Her face showed in a small frame of the canvas flap. "I ain't working today. Sorry, try later."

"I'm not here for that. I came to visit—just talk with you. See if you needed anything."

"Wait. I see who you are. I'll put on a robe."

She wasn't dressed in there? Hell, wasn't everyone up and dressed by this time of day? Guess that showed him what he knew about doves.

In a short while, she opened the flap and invited him in. The light inside was not very bright. The robe she wore was as fine as mosquito screen and near transparent. He must have swallowed twice looking at the slender body underneath it. His Stetson off, he sat on the opposite cot and put his hat on the ground topside down. A cowboy never put his hat on a bed. Give a man ten years of bad luck if he did that.

She bore a black right eye and a blue bruise on her left cheek that he could make out in the shadowy light, but her voice was steady. "Thank you for saving me from another beating this morning."

Norm nodded. "He's in jail."

She swept the long hair back from her face.

"His gang will break him out of there, or he'll get out another way." She looked up at him, made a sour face, and shook her head. "They broke him out of the Hastings jail nine months ago."

"These people act pretty tough."

"Him and his gang are all killers. The best thing for you to do is get on your horse and go back south. He'll want to kill you first off when he breaks out."

"How long have you been with him?"

"He set me up in a tent in Abilene over a year ago."

"He forced you to do this work?"

"Either that or lose all my teeth."

"Kathy Starr isn't your real name then?"

She shook her head and smiled. "Edith Griswald."

"Where did he find you?"

"Headed for our soddy west of the Wichita crossing on the Arkansas River on my wedding day."

"He kidnapped you?"

"Yes. After that he cut my new husband's throat with a bowie knife."

"That was the Griswald?"

"Yes. Poor man, we never shared a bed. We were traveling from our wedding ceremony in a farm wagon back to his homestead. Elder and his gang must have spotted me in my white wedding dress. They stopped him, and Elder told him that he wanted to sample the bride. Wayne flew off that wagon to fight him before I could even stop him. Elder got him in a headlock, then he cut his throat like he was butchering a hog. Next thing Elder left his blood all over my white dress that come off him with us lying in the grass when he consummated my marriage."

Norm couldn't believe that she could say these things in such an offhand way. She had to live with the memories. He guessed she'd come to terms with what had happened the only way she could. He looked up at her and said, "I haven't got much, but you don't have to stay here. I damn sure wouldn't beat you up, and we'd have food and a place of our own. Not any castle, but I would provide you a better life if you have any desires to quit this business."

"What's your name?"

"Norman Thompson."

"Why are you doing this?"

He didn't answer. He wasn't sure himself. Somehow seeing her with that bruise on her face, talking about her husband's cold-blooded murder in that calm voice, like it was no more than she expected or deserved, stirred his heart.

She shook her head, as if she was reading his mind. "I can tell you're a gentleman, but what if some guy from my past came by and recognized me— wouldn't that embarrass you?"

"No. I would treat you like I would a wife from elsewhere."

"You don't understand. It is not the same. A man who paid to lie with me before would think he still had the right to pay me and do it again."

"I won't put up with that."

"Once you've taken money for it, you're never the same again. Even if I had the willpower to decline him, he'd still expect it and take it any way. You'd try to stop him, and he'd kill you like Elder did poor Wayne."

"Edith. I am a man capable of many things. Maybe this reward money could set us up and get us started to having a ranch of our own—somewhere. I am offering you a place in my life as a partner. It's time for you to leave this hellacious business and the two of us live together like normal people do."

"No one's called me Edith in years." She swept her hair back from her face. "I may need to be treated–"

"Treated?"

"Yes. A doctor can do that, they say."

"Oh?" What did she ever mean by that?

"Men can spread diseases to woman in this trade. Then those women spread them to other men. You don't have any of those diseases, do you?"

"No, ma'am, not that I am aware of."

She gave him a faint smile. "Oh, you would know. What will you do next?"

"My only plan was to kick tin cans around here until the reward comes through."

She looked him up and down, as if she was trying to make sure that he wasn't lying to her, wasn't just another hope doomed to be broken. "All right, then. If you will wait for me. I promise that I will come to you. We can try it—us living together. Where are you staying at?"

"I have a tent, too. It's about a mile upstream in the Platte River bottoms from the bridge, on the far side of the river."

"How is your tent marked?"

"It has a N T Bar brand painted on the east side."

"N T Bar? That's your brand?"

"Yes. I had it registered in Texas. Not up here. I didn't need it yet."

"They call you Norman?"

"Or Norm. Thompson is my last name. Call me what you like. When can I expect you?"

"In a few days."

"You want to be married?"

"That isn't necessary. We need some time to get to know each other and how this will work. We may have a real hate relationship after a week." She had a pretty smile when she reached over and squeezed his outstretched hand.

He looked her right in her blue eyes. "No. It won't. I promise you that."

"We'll have time to see all about that. I will be there at your tent in three days, unless things don't follow my plans. But please wait for me?"

"I'll wait for you. You need this stuff moved?"

"I may sell all of it." She rose and kissed his forehead. "You are as sweet and sincere a man as I ever met. God bless you, Norman Thompson of the N T Bar."

He swept up his felt hat. Would she really come to his tent in three days? He would never really know for sure until she came—would he? Damn, that made his stomach roll. Maybe he needed some food. This meeting with her wearing next to nothing had shaken him more than he imagined.

Before he left, she kissed his forehead. The next thing he knew, he was standing outside her tent, trying to make himself believe what had just happened. Not in a million years would he have thought the morning would end this way—not in a million years.

Then a darker thought came to him. Was she simply putting him off to get rid of him? But no, he couldn't believe that. Not after seeing her smile.

CHAPTER No. 2

N ORM HAD NO time to brood, though. He had wandered back down to the Elk Saloon still trying to figure out what he'd gotten himself into, when a reporter named Pfister Malone found him. That was the first thing he said. "Hi, mister, I'm Pfister Malone. I'm a reporter." He stuck out a skinny hand to shake. "Are you the outlaw hunter?"

Norm looked him up and down. A freckle-faced boy, he didn't appear to be out of his teens, in a striped suit coat and sporting an unkempt mane of curly red hair. Malone was armed only with paper and pencil. He followed Norm around, popping questions like popcorn in a hot skillet, while Norm filled his plate off the free lunch counter with fresh sliced bread, mustard, sliced ham and cheese, plus slaw and potato salad, then headed for the table where his beer waited. The aroma of the bread filled his nose with a sweet aromatic flavor that really stuck in his nostrils.

The questions just kept coming, faster than he could answer them.

"Who was the first outlaw you ever captured? Where did you begin your career? How many rewards have you collected? What led you to Ogallala? Did you know Elder was hiding here right under the Ogallala police department's noses? How could I interview Kathy Starr, his alleged mistress?

What was her part in the capture of Elder? I know you are a busy man, but two of his gang members, Tootie Black and Herman Jasper, have four-hundred-dollar rewards on them. Are they next on your list of men to capture?" Then he came back with, "Is there anything you can tell me?"

"Yes," Norm said, trying to curb his impatience. "I am eating my lunch right now. I am entitled to some peace and quiet since I had no breakfast in my camp this morning."

"Why was that?"

"My black servant had to go to a business meeting and had no time for me."

"My heavens what kind of a business meeting did he attend—here?"

He had a mouthful of flavorful food and honestly wanted nothing to do with this auctioneer-style reporter. With a hard shake of his head and a scowl, he told Malone that he had no idea about what the nature of that meeting involved. He took a big sip of sour beer and added, "I have no time today for an interview."

"But, sir, I have a deadline to meet on the newspaper today, or they will—"

"Will what? Shoot you?"

"They might or short my pay, and I could not afford that."

"How much do you make a month?"

"Fifteen dollars."

"Here's fifty cents that will pay for today's loss. Now go." He picked up the other half of his sandwich.

"But—but.... "

"No buts about it. I paid your employment for the day." With that, he took a big bite of his food. Wonderful stuff. Better than answering a bunch of damn fool questions anyhow.

But Malone wasn't going to give up. "Since you won't tell me your purpose or how you do it, can you at least tell me how you got up here to Nebraska?"

"On my ass."

His eyes opened wide. "You rode a mule from Texas all the way?"

Okay, enough of this. "Let me put this to you plain. Shut up with your stupid questions and get out of my life before I shoot you."

At least that much Malone understood. He clamped his lips shut and scrambled away.

Norm finished his sandwich, coleslaw, and potato salad in peace. That boy was more than he could stand.

He checked on his horse and packhorse at the livery and found they were doing fine. Better than staking them out down in the river bottoms and having to water them several times a day. For forty cents they got good hay and had water, and he had a mind free from worry. He'd leave them and hope the reward came quickly. Most of all, he was looking forward to his trial period with Edith to begin. That was almost dreamlike in his mind, such a beautiful woman agreeing to try to be a part of his life. Never mind about what she'd been forced into. He could rescue her from that hell and have a wife in the bargain.

That morning's events were the most unbelievable thing in his entire thirty years, and it had all happened so easily— like it was meant to be.

He went back for supper in a café on Main Street. He'd have to get used to this hiking back and forth. In the past he always rode a horse if he was going anywhere, almost to going across the street. But with his horses boarded in the livery, walking became his chief mode of getting wherever he needed to be.

He was cutting up his chicken fried steak with gravy mashed potatoes and garden fresh green beans, when a burly guy came busting in the café, cleared his throat like a male lion, and asked, "Anyone in here know where that whore Kathy Starr went? She sold her tent to some ugly bitch, and no one knows where the hell she went. Anyone in here know where that whore is hiding her ass?"

"Mister, you just get the hell out of here. There are family people in here. Don't you have any respect?" He stood up, still wearing his napkin bib, and looked the red-faced man right in the face as he pointed at the door for the man to leave.

"Listen you—" But the intruder cut his speech off short when a half dozen guys threw down their napkins, and they stood up too. Immediately, he left, and the bell over the door jangled when he slammed it. One of the men who'd stood gave him a grin.

"Mister, we heard about how you was that famous outlaw hunter and took out Elder with one punch. Figured we'd be better off on your side than that feller's."

Another one drawled, "That's right. Anyhow, 'bout time someone stood up to his kind. Listen at how he talked. Bad upbringing, that's what it is."

A chorus of "Amen," followed his words, and the restaurant crowd resumed eating.

So did Norm. Famous outlaw hunter, again. Guess it was better he had that reputation than a lot of others he could think of. But now, he was worried about Edith. Had she sold her belongings and left? It would be days before her promised arrival at his tent. Had she lied to him, slipped away so she could get far away on her own and set up a tent as a whore somewhere else?

The thought made the good food he had eaten settle like a brick in his belly. This would be a long wait. He felt like the guy who tried to catch a bird with his hands, and all he ended up with was a few feathers. His part of this deal with her had been one sister-like kiss on his damn forehead. When did three days start—was this one of them, or did the time start in the morning?

He wished he'd gotten a better idea of what she was planning. Hell, he should have had her outline it all and sign it. Now, instead of happily waiting for her second coming to him, he would worry the rest of the time she had flown the coop.

S HE MUST HAVE been busy at her trade beforehand, because the next day Norm heard three different men lamenting how she was gone.

They weren't ordinary ranch hands or laborers, either. He saw by their dress they must have had some form of business of their own.

His dark mood got darker when, at midday, he saw the same big man who burst in the café looking for her the night before all dressed up and driving into town in a surrey with a nice-looking woman considerably younger than he was. Obvious as all get out, he had a wife. They went in the mercantile, and Norm decided to do a little snooping. He was behind a counter full of alarm clocks when the clerk said, "Oh, Mister and Missus Clark, what may I get for you this morning."

"That son of a—" But those words only slipped off the edge of Norm's lips in a whisper, and he went back outside. That big-mouthed ape needed his backside caved in with someone's pointed-toed boots. Outside the store, he looked both ways and crossed the street to go have a beer.

The arresting officer, McQuire, spied him from his position in the shade, leaning on a post under the Elk Saloon porch. "You seen his woman at all?"

"What woman?"

"The one he beat up on before you stopped him. You know, Kathy Starr?"

"I haven't seen her since he got through with her," he lied.

"Well, she's missing, and everyone is asking for her. Hell, I have no idea where she went. If Elder had had his way, since she caused the fuss with you and got him captured, I bet today she'd been dead, face down and floating in the Platte River."

"I don't know where she went or is at."

McQuire frowned. "You know, I was thinking, I've been working this part of town, and I never noticed that outlaw Elder in all the time he must have been here. Of course, wanted posters are never good pictures of the wanted men. Ain't like they stood and posed for 'em, know what I mean? But damn it, if I'd even had better eyes for his kind—my wife is so mad over me missing getting that reward she won't sleep with me. Made me sleep on the couch by myself the last two nights."

"I'm real sorry about that. Anything I could do about it?"

"Aw, if she don't let up any soon, I'll get one of them girls out back to treat me till she comes back to her senses."

"I bet they would."

He grinned. "Policemen's rights, I call it."

"How does Elder like the jail?"

"Why, he's a raving idiot. Bragging to us his boys are coming every day to break him out like they did at Hastings. I got news for him. This ain't Hastings, and he ain't getting away."

"I'll keep my eyes open for anything suspicious."

"Good. Two of them bums in his gang, Black and Jasper, have got four-hundred-dollar Wells Fargo bounties on them as well."

"Well, I better get on my way before that reporter finds me. He's a pest."

"He is that. He's figuring that if he gets a big first story on you, he can sell it for a couple hundred bucks to a New York paper."

"That's why he wants it, huh?"

"Sure. He works for nothing, but if they get a big news story break, he can do real well."

Norm went inside, ordered a draft beer, and stood at the bar. He'd learned the bartender's hefty wife was the one who baked the bread, smoked the ham, and sliced the cheese. Plus, they said she grew the onions, cabbage, and the potatoes she used in her salad. He'd watched her setting it up, all dressed up and her hair pinned up neat as can be. The barkeep told him that the guy who owned the saloon paid her fifty cents a day year-round for doing it, and he bought the supplies when her garden ran out in winter.

With her own money, she bought real nice dress material, made her own clothing, and always dressed very well. The lunch counter job made her a cut above most of the women in town.

So, he was back again in the Elk. No place else to go, really. Drank two beers, ate lunch, and worried all afternoon. He figured that was still better than listlessly napping in his tent.

The third day came as slow as Montana molasses in January. But he was up early and left his tent to head to town, cutting through the narrow footpath in the river bottoms that was choked with tall willows. He was jerked out of his own thoughts when he heard the words. "...ucking jail anyway. Hurry up. They change the guards in ten minutes. We've got to be there or wait another twenty-four hours to get him out."

Norm drew his gun and moved slowly in their direction, crouching in the thick tangle of willows, following the sound of their horses tromping just a few feet away. He knew he needed to see them before they saw him. They'd either shoot first or run away, and either way he lost.

Willows parted, he spotted one of the talkers in the saddle with his back to him, and he moved in. "Hands in the air or die."

That man went for his gun. Norm shot him in the back of his head, then took his second shot at the other man on horseback who was facing him. Number two was hit and pitched off his horse. The noise caused the terrified animal to buck, and it collided into number one's mount. Norm was scrambling to get a clear shot at number three, but he had decided to run rather than face the man who'd already shot two of his comrades. He spurred his horse around a corner, but before he disappeared, Norm intentionally shot his pony. The poor horse did an ass over teakettle roll going down first on his knees and then rolled over on top of his screaming rider.

After that, silence reigned, aside from the snorting horses and some of the river bottom women in the distance who had heard the shots and were yelling for help.

Norm knelt and felt the neck of the man he'd shot first for a pulse. Nothing there.

Some boys burst on the scene, wide-eyed with fear and excitement. "Go fetch the law," Norm said. "Tell 'em I've got the Elder gang down here in the river bed all shot up."

He tested the number two man for a pulse. Also, nothing. He straightened and faced the line of curious women holding back their smudge-faced children at the edge of the clearing.

An older woman stepped forward. "Kin we butcher that hoss you's just kilt?"

"Yes, but only the horse."

She laughed aloud at his words. "Bless you, big man. We can make jerky from 'em and have all of us food to eat all winter long."

The crowd clapped and shouted to thank him.

"Them boys go for the law like I told 'em?" he asked.

"Aw, yeah. They've been gone long enough to get there by now."

He agreed. Two horses were alive, so he had acquired three saddles too. Three Winchesters, six guns, and they must have had camping gear. He found a total of seventy dollars in bills and coins in their pockets and more money in their saddlebags that he made sure never to expose to the curious eyes following him around there. The camp folks had been friendly so far, but many a friend turned into an enemy when that much money was involved.

The camp women had already rolled the dead horse over and started skinning it. He added that saddle to the one on the dark horse, the one number one had been riding. More paper money was in those saddlebags, but he only looked at it like it was nothing and strapped it shut.

That was when the law arrived.

"They all dead?" the police chief asked, shaking Norm's hand.

The sheriff, a fat man with a thick mustache, shook his head over the matter. "We'll get the corpses. You get to keep the horses, guns, saddles, and the reward for them. I can see already you're going to live higher than I am for a while."

"How did you get these outlaws?" the police chief asked him.

"I was coming up here through the willows to go to town. They never saw me, but they were talking out loud about busting Elder out of the jail while you changed guards this morning. I decided I better stop them. I ordered them to put their hands up. They went for their guns. The third man was getting away, so I shot his horse. It did a somersault, landed on top, and killed him. That's about it. No one else got hurt."

"Wells Fargo will owe you twelve hundred more. They wanted all three of them. What are you doing next?"

"Wait for my reward, I guess."

"Hey, they may have a parade for you, after all you did."

Norm nodded toward his new horse. "I won't have to worry about having a horse to ride."

"Look for them to do that. Our town likes parades," the chief said.

All the money he found was stashed in his own saddlebags to count later. He took the two horses, three saddles, and gear to town. After several hours dickering with the liveryman, Norm swapped him the two good saddle horses for two hundred bucks and a couple of pack horses. He sold two saddles for sixty and the fancy one with silver for fifty with a pair of pack saddles thrown in. So, before they got busy trading on the outlaws' camp goods, rifles, holsters, and pistols, he had over three hundred bucks in his pocket.

Back at the Elk Saloon, the regulars bought him beers to celebrate his latest captures while he feasted on a big steak and baked potato supper that the free-lunch lady fixed special for him.

It was long past sundown when he came up the bottoms, almost feeling his way under the stars to get back to his camp through the thick willows. He'd reloaded his pistol after the shootout but carried his saddlebags loaded heavy with money on his left shoulder in case he needed to draw his gun. It was a pretty edgy trip for him going back without a light. There were not any more known gang members on the loose, but who knew anything about them, anyway? And Elder's gang wasn't the only bunch of outlaws out there who would like to rob a lone man on foot with money in his bag.

Dogs barked, but otherwise the night was quiet, and nothing threatened him. He undid the tent flap, steeling himself against the disappointment of knowing she wasn't there. It was still tied on the outside. Maybe he had to wait another day—he even prayed for God to send her to him. He lay there on his cot, not sleeping, and fretted about his having all this success without her. Why, he'd pay for the moon to have her. He'd found four outlaws. He was a rich man, after all....

"Norman? Norman? Can you wake up?"

His heart nearly stopped. He reached his hands up, touching soft skin, and then she sweetly kissed his mouth and slipped down in his arms on top of him.

He settled underneath her, reached up and caressed her face. "You've cut your hair?"

"I did several things to cut me off from my past." They kissed.

"But why? It was so lovely long."

"I had it dyed, too. But the doctor says I am free and clean for you. The treatments were severe, but if they did as he said, we should not have any problems." She paused, and he heard the smile in her voice. "You're acting like you doubted I was coming today or was even coming at all."

"Oh, I have had doubts, I guess. Why would a woman as nice as you ever come back for me?"

"I'm here now. I heard you shot three more gang members with bounties on their heads today." She was sitting on top of him unbuttoning his shirt like she owned him and helped him remove it.

"They were planning to raid the jail and get Elder out. I stopped them."

"I'm going to stand up." She stepped off the cot. "Shed your pants. It'll be you and me in this bed on our wedding night—if you can stand me?"

Wedding night? She was serious. He was standing up. His head felt dizzy, and he stripped off his pants. She was nested on her back on top of the cot and held out her arms for him.

What if he disappointed her? There would be no going back. No chance to do it over.

"Real easy," she whispered when their bodies made contact. "I'm excited to be with you, Norman Thompson. Didn't you think I'd do as I promised you I would?"

"Well, I'm sure glad you did. But you only kissed me like my sister kissed me when I left home—"

Her lips against his own drowned out anything else he had to say.

CHAPTER No. 3

NEXT MORNING, EDITH was on her knees at the campfire making flapjacks, and the coffee was boiling on the grill right beside the skillet. "You eat this stack. I'll make more."

Dressed in men's clothing and her short black hair in a Dutch bob, she didn't look anything like Kathy Starr. Her disguise was so good few would recognize her. He couldn't believe, sitting there cross-legged on the ground with molasses dripping off each forkful, that she was really there with him. The Arbuckle's coffee tasted like ambrosia to him, and the wood smoke shifted a little back and forth. If he had to choose between heaven and sitting right where he was in the Platte River bottoms, it wouldn't have been an easy choice.

Ogallala had a parade for him. She stayed out of the spotlight, and he rode with the driver on top of a Wells Fargo Stagecoach behind the marching band. At the end of the ceremony, they gave him a key to the town. The two stayed in the hotel that night. Wells Fargo held a special banquet, and he got all the reward money in a check at the ceremony.

Next day he cashed the check. He bought her a dish-faced single-footing dun horse and a saddle, both her size to ride. Before he left town, he shook all the policemen's hands, and McQuire whispered, "I've seen your wife some-where else besides here."

"Aw, hell, lots of women look alike."

"Not that good-looking, though."

They rode north and made a loop to the east. She rode along with him as if she'd been born to it. She seemed happy to be with him and was a real honeymooner at night. He'd have sure married some gal ten years earlier if he knew life with a woman was going to be this good.

After dinner one night, he told her that. She poked one finger into his belly and said that was why God saved him for her.

He had little doubt about that, either.

The only thing that cast a shadow in his mind was something he wasn't even sure he saw. As they were leaving town, he saw a horseman in the dis-tance, sitting still as a statue. The man was watching them, he was sure of it, even though that far away you couldn't see his eyes. Something in the man's posture made a chill run up his backbone. He was about to spur his horse to turn around, go and confront the man—after telling Edith to stay where she was—when the man turned aside himself and disappeared.

He kept a stiff lookout after that, but they had no trouble, and there was no more sign of the horseman. On their way south, they passed through Baxter Springs, Kansas, a prairie town down near the Indian Territory line, dodging rigs parked haphazardly in the crowded street. They led two pack horses that they'd added, so they could bring along enough comfortable bed-ding and other gear to avoid bedbug ridden hotel beds and bad saloon cook-ing. They plodded down the dusty main street, taking their time. Norm was pleased at the raised eyebrows when they looked at Edith—pleased because she was his.

A familiar voice called out, "Norm Thompson, you old devil, what in the hell are you doing way up here?"

He turned and caught sight of a tall, fresh-faced man dodging through the horses and people on foot trying to catch up with them.

"Who's that?" Edith asked.

"Ike. Ike Andrew. He and I went up the Chisholm trail several times with an old man who liked the two of us." He reined up.

She gave him a mild frown. "What does he do here?"

He turned up his hands and shook his head before he swung off his horse. The pair shook hands, and Ike smiled up at her. "You must be the Missus."

"This is Edith. We're looking for a ranch."

"Lots of them out there. I'm running a steer outfit down on the Cherokee Strip in the Indian Territory. We brought up three thousand long yearlings and two-year-old steers from Texas to finish out up here on this great grass. Wonderful grazing country. They've been doing great."

"No fences?"

"No fences, but brother, it covers that whole Cherokee Strip, which has thousands upon thousands of acres."

"Buffalo gone?"

"Yeah, they shot all of 'em."

"Who holds the leases?"

"A combine of big men from down in Texas, but they will make room for others. Line up some young cattle in Texas and drive them north."

"I can buy a thousand down there for ten or fifteen bucks a head. Put a thousand behind that for help, grub, tents plus cots, and to pay interest on the loan. Hire help. Take some losses, move them to a rail head, and hope to hell I made some money."

Ike's eyes opened wide. "Where you gonna get the money for that?"

"Let's just say I got lucky."

Ike shrugged. "All right, then. Folks have been doing it. Making enough money to go back home and buy a real ranch."

He looked back at his wife.

She threw her hands out at him and smiled. "Hey, you know the cattle business, I'm just riding along."

"Ike, can we put our horses up and hope to get us a clean hotel room? We may need to talk about this some more."

"Sure," Ike said with a grin. "Sounds like you can afford it."

That evening after supper, the three sat on benches on the porch of the Orleans Hotel. Norm explained how he'd struck it rich—and how Edith had come to be his wife. They also discussed the formation of Texas businessmen and ranchers who had organized the Grazing Association of the Cherokee Strip.

"They rented all these acres of this Strip from the Cherokee tribe for grazing cattle. Then they rent it out to others with a low tax for their operation. It goes from west of Fort Supply clear back to almost the Missouri border and starts at the Kansas line, then goes south for a hundred miles. The Kansas state line is its northern border. Water and grass aplenty—it's really a great place for cattlemen to bring stocker cattle, fatten them, and then put them on train cars right over here in Kansas to ship them to market."

"But how many head do you need to make money?"

Ike had his elbows on his knees and leaned more forward in the bench. "Like we took to Abilene and later Wichita. Two thousand head or more."

"Cattle like that in Texas cost what—ten, maybe twenty bucks a head? Then you hire a crew, a cook, a chuckwagon. Get yourself a *remuda* and spend twelve months up here—it gets cold here too, brother—and what can you make?"

"From forty to seventy bucks a head."

"How much does it cost to graze them?"

"Seven-fifty a head for one year."

"That's fifteen thousand dollars for pasture?"

"You can make money at that. Do you see that?"

"I do, but its midsummer now, I couldn't be back here in less than four months with a herd. It would be winter by then."

"Then wait till spring, so you'll have the water on the way up here for the cattle."

"Edith? What do you think?"

She'd been listening carefully. Here was a woman who wasn't afraid to understand men's business and give her opinion, too. "If you can get the finances. Try it. You say you've driven them before successfully."

"But never grazed and played nursemaid to them for twelve months. Could you stand it?"

She smiled and nodded her head. "Remember, Norm. I have stood much worse things in my life."

"The damn wind blows all the time up here," He looked hard at her for her preferences.

"You trying to talk me out of it or yourself?" She looked over at Ike. "Don't worry, Mister Andrew. We go through this a lot."

"If you could put up with me, I'd listen a damn sight better to you than he does." Ike grinned and waggled his eyebrows.

She laughed. "No. Trust me, I love him. This is our game."

"How do I get a permit?" Norm asked.

"Fill out a form. Get it passed by the board and pay a grazing fee."

"Say for now, I bring two thousand head."

"I can find out for you tomorrow. Then, if you're going south, come by my camp down on the Cimarron River, and you can see my operation. Hell, I'll stay here overnight and ride south with you two. Sorry, ma'am, for cussing. I don't have a wife, but those boys will be glad to see you."

They wound up their discussion, said good night to Ike, and went to bed on the hotel's fresh wind-dried sheets—crisp and clean smelling after a hot bath and him a shave. He knew he'd have to sleep in less comfortable quarters if he succeeded at what he was going to attempt, but for now, may as well enjoy it.

THE NEXT MORNING, Norm watched Edith getting dressed with a smile on his face. "You miss anything from your former life?"

She paused in pulling on her britches. "Not very much of anything. I'm now real saddle tough. I can ride all day and not ache one bit, and I enjoy the new country opening up. You fret about me, and that is real nice, after my past life. I like everything about our deal. Being with you is nice, and you never get mad or cross at me. That is an entire new world to simply live in. No man is demanding me or hurting me. No one hitting me for no reason and expecting for me to submit in any way he chooses." She finished dressing, saying, "I hope you can stand me a lot longer. There is no place I'd rather be than with you."

"That makes two of us who are satisfied, Edith."

Later that day, he learned the setup fee for his venture was seven dollars and fifty cents a head, non-refundable. He put his money up and signed the agreement. The office clerk said the agreement would be passed since Ike had vouched for him. The rent started when he arrived there with cattle.

The next morning, they headed south with Ike. It was on one of the old cow trails that came out of Texas to reach the Kansas railroad depots where they shipped them east. The grass was deep and rich, and the whole scene impressed him with its vastness and beauty.

Meadowlarks and killdeer were everywhere, and they even flushed some prairie chickens. An occasional deer ran off in the passing miles. Red-tailed hawks screamed at the pair as if they were invaders, and buzzards drifted by to observe a possible death discarded. He knew this bluestem grass was a rich cattle-ranching country. All he had to do was find a Texas banker smart enough to partner with him.

Norm glanced around. "The buffalo are all gone?"

"No one's seen one." Ike laughed. "You and I have seen lots of them, though, haven't we?"

"That was on those first drives we made up here to sell cattle."

"There were some here when we went north, was it five years ago?" Ike asked. "They may be a few left out here. It's large country east to west and even north to south. I saw a zebra once, in west Texas, running loose. Cowboys caught him, but he kicked and bit them so bad they finally turned him loose. No one ever saw him again or knew where he came from."

Ike's zebra tale had Edith laughing and shaking her head. "Cowboys have such funny stories. Look, Mom! A zebra."

"I'll tell you. I really did see three camels in west Texas and some Arab driving them."

She burst out laughing again. "Where were they going?'

With his big grin, Ike shook his head. "Maybe Bethlehem. Hell, Edith. I don't speak Arab talk."

"Did you two pull tricks on everyone on those drives?"

"Oh, a few," Ike said. "If you help him coming back with the cattle, you'll see how boring a cattle drive can be. First few days, they break rank like drafted soldiers and try to run away, but in a few days all they ever know is follow that tail ahead of them. Sort of like Norm here. He just keeps moving on, even when he's asleep."

Norm rode in and clapped his hand on her leg. "Honey, didn't you know that cowboys can sleep in the saddle and never fall out?"

"I don't doubt either of you. It simply is funny. Before I met Norman, no one laughed in my world about the funny things. The people in that world laughed at giving others real pain. I mean they laughed at something really hurting someone. So, I enjoy your wild tales."

"Where were you?" Ike asked.

Norm frowned and started to answer, but Edith stopped him with a little shake of her head.

"It's okay, Norm." She turned to Ike. "I was the slave-prisoner of a mean man. He was beating me in an alley for some infraction of his law when Norman stopped him."

"I can see that happening, and I would have expected Norm to do that to anyone beating up on a woman."

"He did. He knew the beater would kill him for doing it, and he didn't aim for that to happen."

Ike nodded. "Texas cowboys are tough when they're backed to the wall."

With her pretty smile, she said, "Real tough but funny, too."

"You didn't know you had such a smart lady?"

Norm reined his horse back a little. "I know one thing. I had a wonderful Christmas in August back in Ogallala getting her to ride away with me."

"Hey, Edith, you get hold of your twin and send her to me, okay?" Ike said.

"No twin. Two sisters, though, but last thing I knew, they were married and happy."

"How about cousins?"

She laughed again.

Two days later they reached his headquarters. The pens and raw lumber sheds along with corrals were set up in a wide valley. His horse herd was cared for by wranglers, and the large canvas tent had tables to feed the crew, and the cook's kitchen shelter was in another.

His foreman, Johnny Bailey, met them, and the Chinese cook, Ho Chu, served them large pieces of raisin and dry apple pie with their coffee. The windswept tables were scrubbed clean, and the camp looked neat under the canvas covers flapping in the wind. Ike had a dozen hands that each day rode the range's perimeters and basically turned their cattle back to their region.

Ranchers did that in Texas, but it required some hard riding and no sleeping under a shade tree around some water hole during the daytime. Still, it was all worth it to see his dream coming true.

F ROM THERE, THEY rode on south.

"Have you been thinking who you are going to talk to about this loan for those cattle you'll need?" Edith asked.

"I know a few in San Antonio. One guy in particular. Alan Adams. Cross your fingers for me."

"Maybe pray, too."

"That would not hurt. I prayed to get you. Those three days I waited for you were really long."

"I wanted to be with you, too, but I told you I was coming."

He rode in close and kissed her cheek. "I love you, pretty lady. You came along with me, and now we need—I need thousands of dollars to finance a poker game."

"Is it as wild as poker, what you plan?"

"Darling, any time you borrow money and mix that with cattle sales a year later, you're playing poker."

"I see. Well, if I can help, I will do what you need of me."

"I appreciate you. We can win this war. I didn't put up over a thousand dollars of our money to simply lose it."

The next day, they stopped in the settlement in the Strip called Government Springs. He winked at her before he dismounted to hitch their horses, then he gave her a head toss to go shop for her needs inside the store. The place looked familiar. It was the same location where he'd watered his herds while moving them north, a few years earlier.

"Let's get what supplies we need here and move on today."

"Certainly." Her face changed, becoming guarded. "Wait, Norm." She pulled him back by the sleeve behind their horses. In a whisper in his ear she said, "That man on the porch is wanted. The bearded one. Don't look now. He's a killer, too."

"You go by me and get inside the store. His name?"

"Daily. Watch out for him." Her frown showed concern and indicated that he sure must be bad.

"Go ahead."

She nodded, resumed a smile as if nothing was wrong, and went up the stairs past the two men without giving either a look. The outlaw on the right of his pal frowned and glanced at her disappearing in the door.

Norman, by then, was beside him. He slipped his six-gun out and shoved the muzzle in the outlaw's guts. "Both of you raise your hands. I'll shoot you if you make one wrong move. Daily, I hear you're wanted dead or alive."

He jerked the man's gun out of his holster and stuck it in his waistband. "Both of you start down the stairs. Careful. I damn sure will shoot you before you get one step."

"Who in the hell are you?"

"A bounty hunter, and you better to listen to my orders." He disarmed the second man. "Now get down on your knees."

He made them kneel and then lay face down on the ground.

She came out and moved through a crowd of curious hushed men and women gathered on the porch. "Here is some rope. Figured you'd need it."

His voice low, he asked, "He got any help you see in there?"

"No."

"Find the local law or where we can take them."

"I can get that done."

When he finished tying both of their hands behind their back, he straightened and asked, "Where is the law?"

"He's coming." A woman under a sunbonnet pointed out a tall hatless man coming down the dirt street in a jog.

Catching his breath, the lawman, a red-faced man in his thirties, frowned at Norman as if he couldn't believe what he was seeing.

Norm pointed. "These men are wanted. I arrested them. I also want the bounties on them."

"I ain't wanted," the second man complained.

"We'll see about that," the lawman said. "My name's Tom Byres. I have a jail about a quarter mile west of here. I'm the deputy sheriff in this area."

"Tom, my name is Norman Thompson. I'm going back to Texas with my wife. We recognized Daily, there, and I arrested him and his associate, who I have no doubt is wanted, too."

They stood the two up.

"I don't recognize either of them, but I trust you know him."

"Daily. That's who he is."

"I don't know how in the hell you know me. Must be that bitch with you." Daily shook his head. "She looked familiar to me,"

"You say one more word about that lady, and I'll knock your teeth out, and you'll gum your food in prison."

"And I'll turn my back and let him do it to you," Tom said and shoved them to move.

"I'll go with you," Norm said.

"No, take care of your wife. Then ride down there, and we'll fill out the papers. They won't escape me."

"Thanks, Tom. Nice to meet you."

Norm caught up with his wife back in the store and, under his breath, thanked her. "Where did Daily come from?"

"He rode with Elder on some raids they made. I didn't know the second man, but I bet there is a reward on him, too."

"Every hundred dollar reward we collect is that much less we need, huh?"

She nodded, smiled and squeezed his hand, "We're doing fine."

"Let me go back outside and check on which horses they rode in on. We can keep 'em."

"Anyone see what horses that Daily rode in on?" he asked in a loud voice inside the store.

"That bay horse and the sorrel one." One man took him to the front door and pointed them out on the hitch rail. "That guy with him is Haley Blaine. The U.S. Marshal in Van Buren, Arkansas, wants him for robbery and murder. You're sure a tough guy. I wouldn't have touched arresting those two by myself—they're real bad outlaws."

"I know, but someone has to do it."

"You with the law down there?"

Norm shook his head. "Just a citizen doing my duties."

"I bet you find a lot more of 'em going south. That Indian Territory is packed full of them as a sardine can."

"Thanks." Norm nodded to Edith. He went out to examine the two horses, and she headed toward the town's mercantile store to shop.

The sorrel was a good-looking horse, probably stolen. Most outlaws rode more nondescript horses than this particular one. The bay was sound-looking, but had a mean shift in his eyes. He'd probably kick or bite a man if he ever had half a chance. Saddles were common, but the money he found in the sorrel horse's saddlebags were new gold coins. Twenty-dollar ones near the size of a silver dollar. He didn't count them, but they must have come from a robbery somewhere. Good thing these bandits he was finding weren't broke. They'd been real busy at their work.

When she came out with two cloth bags of supplies she'd bought, she asked him what he'd found.

He leaned in close. "Gold coins that shine real bright. I'll pack that stuff you bought in our panniers."

"How many coins?"

"Maybe a hundred or more."

A slow sly smile split her soft lips. "Enough to buy a cow herd?"

"Maybe, maybe more. I'll tell you later tonight when we make camp somewhere and there ain't no extra eyes around."

They damn sure had hit a streak of good luck.

Norm set the bags down, undid the diamond hitch, took back the tarp, and put them away.

"Watch that bay horse." He pointed. "He's got an eye for evil things."

"Really?"

"Trust me. He'll bite, cow kick you, or outright kick you. Stay clear of him."

"You looked in his saddlebags yet?"

"No, and don't try. I'll check him later."

"Wonder where the money came from?"

"A train robbery, maybe. Who knows? But the other guy is wanted, too, by the U.S. Marshal in Van Buren, the old man said. You have five dollars?"

"Sure, why?"

"I want to tip him for helping me."

She found three paper dollars and two silver ones in her purse. He took the bags back to the clerk and then located the older man who told him some more about the outlaws. He took his hand, put the money in his palm, and smiled. "Here is a little tip for helping me."

"Why, hell, you don't owe me nothing."

"Take it, anyway. I appreciate you."

"What's your name, cowboy?"

"Norman Thompson, of Texas."

"Albert Tankersly. Proud to meet you. And thanks for the money."

"No problem. See you again someday. I'll be back up here next year with a herd somewhere in the spring. Find me, and you'll have a job."

"You've got a deal. I'll find you, Mister Thompson."

"Norman. No mister, Albert."

He left him and hurried to his wife. She had the sorrel on a lariat to lead him but had obeyed him and left the bay hitched.

"Albert's his name. You did good. I'll get you the other pack horses' leads."

THE JAIL AT Government Springs looked like a shack. Norm worried it might not hold the pair, but the jailer—his name was Tom— had them each in a leg iron chained to an iron ring in a huge block of concrete inside their cell.

Tom handed Norm the money he'd took from the captured outlaws. Seventy bucks was all they had. Norm handed the money back and told him to count it as his part for caring for them until the law came. He also informed Tom that the U.S. Marshal in Van Buren, Arkansas, wanted Bailey.

He filled out the paperwork, feeling anxious to get away, and asked Tom to mail his rewards to Alan Adams at the First Texas National Bank in San Antonio, Texas. Adams would hold the script he expected from the Marshals Service and deposit the Wells Fargo check in his First National Bank account.

Tom thanked him for the money he paid him and said he would do as instructed about the rest.

When Norm rounded behind the horses to untie them at the hitch rail, he was so anxious to get going, he passed too close behind the bay horse. Sure enough, it kicked him. It wasn't a full-fledged kick, but it knocked him to the ground.

Lying on the ground holding his lower calf where the hoof struck him, he cursed the horse and its former owner. "Damn you, outlaw."

Edith was there in a flash. "You all right?"

"I'll live." He struggled to sit up and jerked his head toward the bay. "But he may not."

"Can you ride?"

"Sure."

She pulled him to his feet with a grin. "Don't you listen to your own damn warnings?"

Once he brushed the dust off his clothes, he kissed her, then sorted out the horses so that he led the bay.

They rode south. It was painful riding with his bruised leg, and when they stopped by a stream later in the day, she watered the other horses and hobbled them. He limped around with the bay and finally had him hobbled and turned out.

She gathered wood and made the fire, then cooked the meal. He lay on his bedroll, trying not to pay attention to the pain. While they ate, she boiled tea from willow bark for him to drink after they finished the meal. She promised him relief and told him that outlaws treated wounded gang members with that kind of tea. It helped ease them, and it would sure relieve him.

Norm drank it, and in a short while, he could stand the pain better. He thanked her for the help.

"Are you going to be able to ride tomorrow?" she asked. "We should have stopped and let you rest it."

"No. I've been hurt worse. Moving puts us further down the road. We need to keep moving. Those two get a chance to tell their buddies on the outside that we have all their money, maybe we'll get chased back to Texas."

"What can we do about it?"

"I think, find a Wells Fargo office and ship all this money to the San Antonio Bank. Then keep moving. Even so, I'm not certain that will end the danger. Anyhow, what we have now is way too much money to pack that far."

"Where will we stop?"

"There's a town called Clermont somewhere south of here. They should have a Wells Fargo service available there. We may be several days getting there, but I think that will be our best bet."

"I can handle all but loading the panniers."

"I'll get them on for you. I'm sorry. I knew better than to trust that damn bay horse."

"If that's all that you ever do wrong, I forgive you. These past days have been the greatest of my life. Now, I know how slaves feel who have gotten freed. You don't know how bad my life back there was minute by minute."

"Don't think about that. Think about what we have now."

"What we have now is all I want." She smiled. "What about you, Norm? Are you happy?"

"Except for that horse kicking me, I wouldn't trade my life with a king."

She dropped on her knees and kissed him hard. "Norm. I'm so very happy."

After eating and stoking the fire, they turned in for the night. On his back in the bedroll, his leg still ached, but he could stand that.

He started thinking about his unexpected career as a bounty hunter. How many people now had a reason to kill him?

He had a way of putting himself at risk, there was no doubt about that. And the outlaws he captured weren't the only ones who had reason to have it in for him. Even back in Montana, he remembered a busted girth that got him thrown, and when he looked at it, it had looked frayed, as if a knife had weakened it. Was that an accident, a mistake, like the bay horse kicking him? Or was it something more?

He thought about what he'd seen that day, seen for the third time just before evening fell—a rider at a distance following them, who, when he turned to get a better look, fell back and vanished. Was it the same man he'd seen when they were leaving Ogallala? No way to tell. Maybe the rider was someone who had nothing to do with him, but his sense told him different. He also knew that, if it did mean trouble, and he came for Norm in this shape, he'd be like a wounded animal, unable to escape. He'd been so busy since

Ogallala with her—he wouldn't tell her now about this concern. She had enough to worry about getting them south across this prairie.

He had known that the bay horse would kick someone, and still he'd let his own guard down. If the man who was following them meant harm, he couldn't make that same mistake again.

CHAPTER No. 4

CLERMONT'S STREETS PROVED to be a muddy slop yard. The busy center of the small town's business district was in a boomtown building stage, churning up the mud and leaving the roads rutted and uneven. To avoid the sea of slop, he turned up a lesser alley and came around into the back of the livery.

As they rode up between the pens, a man came out of the barn alleyway to greet them at the backside of the raw lumber barn with a smile. "Welcome to Clermont, the soon-to-be new capital of the Oklahoma Territory."

Norm stepped down but motioned to Edith to stay in the saddle. "My name is Norman Thompson. From the look of it, they should have called it Mudville instead. Is there a bank on this side of the mud river?"

Two shots cracked the air, and Norm's hand shot for the butt of his gun. "What was that?"

The livery man shrugged. "Hell, that shooting goes on all the time. Cutting down on the population, I guess. My name's Hanson, call me Tye."

"Nice to meet you. The bank?"

"Oh, yeah. Stockman's is on this side of the street. I bank there. See Hal Brooks, he's the main man. You can tell him I sent you."

"Does he have a Wells Fargo transfer service here?"

"Oh, yes. You need to deposit money?"

"No, send it to my bank in Texas."

"Sure. It will cost you, but Hal can handle it."

"I understand fees. Put our horses and gear up, if you will, please. We'll do our banking then come back and get her things or send help after them. Oh, watch the bay horse, he kicks and bites. That's why I've got a bum leg."

He went hobbling back to her on the dun, helped Edith down onto the straw mat in the alleyway. Then he hefted both the heavy saddlebags on his shoulder.

Tye waved a hand at him. "Hey, Norman. Let one of my boys carry that money. You have a bad leg, no need to make it worse. Hey, Jim!" he called. "Come help this man with his bags!"

A big stout teenager came on the double and lifted the bags with a grunt. The boy took a saddlebag over each shoulder. "Whew, bet your horse appreciates getting this off him."

"I imagine so. I'm Norm, she's Edith. Thank you much for your help. You lead the way to the Stockman's Bank."

"I can wait for you. Them other boys get to unload your horses. They may have it done when I get back."

They walked through the livery barn that smelled of strong horse piss out into the daylight and down the boardwalk. Ahead, he saw the bank, housed in a formidable-looking red brick building. Jim followed them in, still bearing the bags.

A teller behind a grill frowned at him as he approached.

"What's your business?" His tone wasn't overly friendly, but Norm figured they saw all types in here, including bank robbers and other outlaws.

"Mister Brooks, please. Tye Hanson sent me."

The teller nodded, said a word in an errand boy's ear, and in a moment, a large man came out into the lobby and gave them a welcome. They made introductions and went into his office, Jim still following packing the two saddlebags on his shoulders.

"Sorry about the mud," Norm said, looking at the tracks the three of them had made walking in.

Brooks waved it off. "The mud's bad. The summer rain is not. Think nothing of it. What can I do to help you?"

"Mister Brooks, I need my cattle proceeds shipped by Wells Fargo to my bank in San Antonio."

Brooks smiled. "Set those bags on the floor, young man. We can handle it from here."

Jim nodded shyly and set the bags down. Norm thanked him and gave him a quarter, then sent him on his way back to the livery.

"How much money do you have?"

"With my rewards from capturing outlaws and the cattle proceeds, over five thousand dollars. We haven't had any good place to count it. I know packing that much money isn't safe, so we stopped off here to let you handle it."

"Wise of you—and something we often need to do. My depositors all farm or raise livestock, so a lot of money can change hands quickly. I'll have two of my tellers count it. We can give you a receipt if you don't want to stand around and watch them."

"No need in that. How much is the fee?"

"Insured and all, I imagine around two hundred dollars. We take a small percentage out of that. Does that sound fair enough?"

He looked at Edith, who nodded silently. "Fine. We need a bath, a meal, and a hotel room. Got any suggestions?"

"I will have a rickshaw take you to Sherman Hotel. These Chinamen make it fine through the mud and will get you over there without a drop of it."

"Serious?"

"I use one every day."

"When should I come back?"

"Two o'clock now. Oh, how about four?"

"Thanks. I'll rest better knowing it is all in good hands."

"The best, sir. The very best."

They shook hands. Brooks said it was good to meet them and thanked them for their business. He sent a teller out to secure them a rickshaw. Minutes later, a barefoot Asian was hauling them to the hotel three blocks away and across the street, making it there without a spill despite going in and around some large rigs on their way to the porch of the Sherman.

He paid the man fifty cents. At the sight of the coins he thanked them wildly in his native tongue, none of which Norman understood.

"They must not pay them much," Edith said under her breath.

Their lodging was quickly arranged, along with a hot bath for them both in their room. A boy was sent to the livery to get the things they'd told Tye Hanson they'd come back for later. A housekeeping lady even ironed a dress for Edith to wear to supper. Norm planned to celebrate their arrival and the deposit of their wealth to be safely shipped to San Antonio. He was in such good spirits, he was even able to ignore the pain in his injured leg for a while.

From the second story hotel window, he studied the street and watched men hold up the hem of their britches and wade the sloppy mess in the street to cross it. He shook his head and laughed.

Busy brushing her hair, Edith shook her head. "What's so funny?"

"How people deal with the mud in Clermont."

"Are you going back to check on the deposit?"

"Yes. You stay here. Our dinner reservations are at six."

She hurried over in a rustle of her dress and petticoats to kiss him. "I can't tell you how good it feels to be in this dress. I know I have to look inconspicuous when riding with you, but it just makes me feel like a woman again."

"What was that word?"

"Inconspicuous. It has nothing to do with my past, that's for sure. It means I blend in with you and the horses in men's clothing. In other words, no one notices me except for you, which is how I want it."

"You look prettier than a picture in that dress."

She smiled and swirled the hem of her skirt. "You be careful and don't get shot. They need a tough town marshal to close all that shooting down."

"I'm not worried. Hell, in Abilene, when it was the railhead, you couldn't sleep at night it was so bright at midnight."

She frowned. "Why was that?"

"Because those damn wild Texas cowboys shot so many holes in the sky."

She laughed. "I love you, big man."

They kissed, and he went to see about the bank business.

Brooks met him in the lobby, and they went back to his office. He handed Norm a piece of paper with the tally, $6,673 written on it.

Almost seven thousand bucks. And that didn't count the five hundred in folding money in his boot vamp hideout, or the two hundred he gave Edith to put in her purse for an emergency. The outlaws had been good to him and Edith. Why, this would all but set them up. And with this much in the bank, he could easily borrow more if he needed to.

"What are your plans?" Brooks asked.

"I have already paid to graze cattle on the Strip next year."

"How many, if I may ask?"

"Two to three thousand head. Depends on what I can find to buy down there in Texas."

Brooks gave him a calculating look. "I've been thinking, Mister Thompson... I'd like to be a partner with you. Buy, say a thousand head. What would they cost?"

"Best I can tell at long distance, ten to twenty dollars a head, then a good year's grazing before taking them to market. I'd split the bills for expenses with you if I can get your cattle bought."

"You buy them and graze them, and we can split on what my cattle bring after expenses. I can furnish the money for you to buy them."

Norm stuck his hand out. "You have a deal. When I get back to Texas and set up a mailbox, I'll be in contact with you. How much do I owe you?"

"A hundred fifty, now that we're partners. They guaranteed the delivery to your bank in two weeks. Is that satisfactory?"

"Sounds terrific."

"Are you and your lovely wife having dinner this evening?"

"I have reservations for six o'clock at the hotel restaurant. Can you join us?"

"Madelyn and I will join you, if you'd like for us to do that."

"Indeed I would. I am certain Edith would love that, too. She's been horseback a long time getting here, and I'm sure she'd like another lady to chat with."

"Well, that's settled, then. I'll have them make you a receipt, and we can talk more at supper."

Two more shots sounded outside. Norm turned his ear toward the sound—there were no more after them.

Brooks shook his head angrily. "I know we need a gun law in this town.

We've needed one for a while, but even if there was one, there's no one to enforce it."

Norm held his hands up defensively. "I punch cattle, not ruffians."

"You mentioned rewards in that amount. You must do a lot of work at that, then?"

"Some is more like it. I don't do it regular."

"A lot of money in that business, if you survive it. Don't blame you for switching to cattle." Brooks smiled. "See you at six."

NORM AND EDITH met Hal and Madelyn Brooks in the lobby at a little before six. Norm gave Brooks's wife a curious look.

Madelyn was definitely a finishing school lady, a little out of place in a rough town like Clermont. She was, Norm guessed, at least ten years younger than Brooks, blonde, with a nice smile, but had a fussy manner that made him wonder how she'd gotten out here in Oklahoma Territory. Norm considered her on the chubby side, but she wore so much dress he couldn't really tell. No appeal to him, anyway. She and Edith could converse, though.

He knew, by this time, his own wife'd been educated higher than himself by the big words he caught in her speech. It didn't bother him—actually, he liked it that he'd picked a smart woman—but he also knew that half of what came to her mind never made it out of her mouth, so she was probably smarter even than he realized. Maybe her imprisonment had silenced her some. Heaven knows, anyone with any sense would keep their mouth shut in that situation. Still, he was glad she was there to share a lot with him and add to his own thoughts on business matters.

When they were all seated for supper, Brooks gave him an appraising eye. "Tell me where all you have been."

"I took cattle up north in '68, a year or so after they opened the Chisholm Trail. After we got there, I spent the summer learning how to swim and cross a river."

"You did *what?*"

"There's fourteen rivers to cross between San Antonio and Abilene. Every damn one scared this dry-lot Texas boy to death. But when I rode back home that fall, I could swim any river I come to. I decided if rivers would keep me from ever being a real drover and taking herds north, I'd learn how to swim 'fore I left Kansas."

"You didn't learn to swim as a boy?"

"There ain't much water over knee-deep west of Fort Worth."

"So you became a cattle-driving hand."

"Yes, sir. I told some folks I could get their cattle to Abilene. Next year, I did, and I was glad I learned how to swim, I didn't realize that was only the beginning of what I had to learn. I wasn't a good boss then. I let people who didn't know a damn thing about how to do things tell me my business, and that got me in some scrapes I didn't need. Like an outfit was dogging along ahead of my herd north of the Arkansas River. We kept holding back, until a bunch of my hands said we could run our herd right through them and go on. That was a mistake that cost me two weeks sorting those two herds of cattle out. That ain't easy without corrals."

Brooks chuckled. "What else did you learn?"

"Don't herd anything out of Texas that ain't a good steer two years or more older."

"Why's that?"

"Buyers up there culled young cattle, and you'd only get two bucks a head for them to feed them to hogs. They'd drive them in a pen, shoot them, step off their horse, gut them open with a Bowie knife, and let the hogs eat them."

Madelyn looked appalled. Brooks just shool his head. "Why do that?"

"Those Illinois buyers want big-framed cattle in their lots for three to four months eating corn, then they go to Chicago as prime beef. Those calves keep growing on corn and don't get fat. So, you waste your time even bringing them up there. I've seen ranchers mad as hornets with buyers culling them all out."

Brooks looked impressed. "All right. There's no market for those yearlings in railheads like Abilene was back then. I'm learning. What else happened?"

"Some crooked gamblers shot two of my men up there over cards. It was a frame-up deal. Hell, they were just boys, and when the gamblers went to losing using their own marked cards, they got mad. They shot them without a chance. I got word and ran them down up on the Republican River. They admitted they had marked cards, and the boys were beating them. One gambler said, 'We got pissed and shot them, thinking that if they admitted it, we'd say we understood why they'd done it and let them go.'"

"I'm guessing you didn't do that."

"Hell, no. I tossed a rope over a cottonwood limb and told them to start praying, because they didn't have long on this earth. They begged us to spare them, right up to the moment the ropes pulled tight. We hung them and left them there for the crows to pick their eyeballs out."

"What they deserved, in my opinion."

"Too much of that kind of thing out there to let anyone get away with it. It was a rough place then, and it's still a rough place. Going back to Texas, I guess some robbers thought I was carrying the cattle sale money home. That was my third year, second one with me as the trail boss. We had just crossed into the Indian Territory, right south of the damned Arkansas River they jumped us. About half the holdup men were Injuns plus some renegade white men who held us up in camp. They wanted the money. They stripped me of my clothes and turned their backs on me standing there buck-naked to challenge my other men to get them to tell them where the money was at or they'd strip 'em and kill 'em just like they was going to do with me.

"My holster and gun were on the ground. I dove for it and used it still in the holster. The first bullet opened the bottom of the holster. My pistol cut down three, wounded another one who started off, but my man, Bill Dawes from Waco, shot him three times before he fell down—tough damn Indian. We hung the wounded one and left the rest for the crows. Didn't take ten minutes to do it all."

"My friend, you have seen some hard times on the trail." Brooks looked impressed, but his wife still had her mouth pinched in a little twist as if she disapproved even of hearing about such matters.

"It never was easy. We took a thousand open heifers to Nebraska. Of course, they weren't all open, and every morning we had to kill day old calves. That got damned old in a hurry, but it had to be done. I knew it would happen when I took the job and charged them for making my men do it."

"You won't bring heifers back, then?"

"Lord, no. But enough about cattle driving. How did you get in the banking business up here?"

"My father was a banker in Missouri. Kansas City. I came down here when they platted this out as a town, got a house lot and the bank lot. Did business in a wooden shed and finally got this brick bank built. We're doing good business, and my business grows. Railroad ever gets here, we'll soar." Brooks gave him a smile. "What are your plans, then?"

"I'll go back to Texas, get a place and start buying cattle. It'll be an all winter job, getting a chuck wagon, remuda, cook, and all the gear we will need for that next year, plus gathering some good hands. All you will get to ride are kids these days. Getting so men ain't leaving their woman's side, not that I can blame them. But I will find them. Get us a nest too. Even though I can't imagine I could make her stay home."

Edith smiled. "I'm going along."

"Where is that?" Madelyn asked.

"Norman's bringing a herd back up there to the Strip next spring. I may be the cook's helper, but I will be there."

That disapproving pinch came back. "You would spend your summer up there in a cow camp?"

"Honey, if you had lived where I did before he pulled me out of there, a cow camp would seem as heavenly a place as you ever stayed in."

Finally, Madelyn showed an emotion other than distaste. Her brow wrinkled in sympathy. "Oh, my God, I am so sorry."

"No need to be. I am not there now, thanks to Norman—enough said."

"How long you two been together?" Brooks asked.

"Two-three weeks, it doesn't matter. We love each other, and I am perfectly happy to be anywhere he wants to go."

"I thought you two had been married to each other for several years."

Norm looked over at Edith and smiled. "The time doesn't matter. We know we're together. It'll work."

"I guess it will."

In the hotel bed later the matter of Norm's sore leg was much improved. Hugging his wife he recalled Brooks's confidence in the plan. Damn right, the cattle drive to the Strip would work. Norm would see to that.

CHAPTER No. 5

THEY LEFT CLERMONT a week later riding south, crossed the
Canadian and Red Rivers, and, after a long week and half, arrived in
Ft. Worth. They stayed in the stockyard district at the Brown Hotel,
and Norm rounded up some out-of-work bachelors he knew were good
enough hands, paid them ten apiece and told them to meet him in two weeks
in Kerrville—he'd have work for them.

He found a few more at Austin in the stockyard district heading south
and paid them to join him at Kerrville. So, he'd have a roster of men to start
with. She wrote them all down in her neat, precise handwriting:

Gunny Johnson
Cabe Forest
Alfred Charles
Roby Hindsman
Cur Taylor
Burt Randal
Harry Zheman
Rowdy Kimmel
Thomas Comack

Then in Austin:

Wylie Carlton
Phil Doone
Prairie McCarty

A week later, when they got to the Crockett Hotel in San Antonio, they were again discussing the hands they'd hired. To Norm's amazement, he discovered that Edith not only knew all the names by heart, she could describe any of the men on the list and knew where they'd come from and where they'd been hired. He could not imagine having a memory like that. But he realized that, unlike most women, she had dealt with men in a way most never have to and had learned to figure out a man quick for her own protection. You had to size people up quickly and remember their faces—because the bad ones would come around again, sure as anything.

He remembered how she'd recognized that outlaw, Daily, up at Government Springs. No hesitation—she'd known who he was. Now, he could expect it from her, and a really useful skill it was, too.

They took baths in the room, had a nice night's sleep, and then breakfast in the restaurant. He bought her two new dresses and ordered her a pair of new cowboy boots custom-made to fit her. Then they went to see his banker, Alan Adams, at the First National Bank.

He met them in the lobby and shook his hand, bowed to her, and took them into an office with longhorn hide couches and chairs.

Adams gave him an impressed smile. "Tell me about all this money you had sent here in your name. I was shocked you did that well up there."

"Some is bounty money for wanted criminals. I captured some of them, shot some, and Wells Fargo paid me well for delivering them," Norm said, seating himself on the couch next to Edith. "Then we arrested some outlaws who had some money, and that became mine. Plus, there should be some rewards sent here and a federal marshal script."

Adams nodded. "The check from Wells Fargo for the two men you rounded up was a thousand, and the script was five hundred for both, but it has to be cashed when the money comes in on the federal bank account on that paper."

"You can handle that?"

"Yes. We'll be the party notified, and we will deposit the money in your account, but it may be six months or longer. They pay slowly."

"I knew that. I'll use some of my money, but I'll need probably forty thousand dollars to go back with those cattle next spring to the Strip. Can you loan it to me?"

"Oh, I'm certain we can. What else?"

"Have you foreclosed on any good ranches lately?"

Alan sat back in his chair and tented his fingers. "The Rocking Chair. You know it. Belonged to Farley Mosey who died of a heart attack last year. His wife spent all the money in his safe and came by with a young man on her arm and told us it was ours."

"How much is against it?"

Alan shook his head. "Way more than i's worth. We know we're going to take a bath. To you, twenty thousand."

"Ten thousand?"

"I'd go to the bank board and ask them if they'd accept that for the ranch." He turned to Edith. ""What do you think? A ranch of our own?"

"Let's talk in private a minute if Mister Adams doesn't mind."

Adams nodded. "Certainly, Missus Thompson. I will step right outside the room."

"Thanks." She smiled and turned back to face Norm when the door closed.

"I have somewhere around ten thousand dollars I salted away over the years. It's sewn in my purse lining. You and I are in this together now. What's mine is yours."

Norm stared at her, then broke out in a grin. "At times, you shock me. But I like being given that kind of shock. We'll make a bid at fifteen. Unless— honey, I know this place. It's a palace with great land and water. We may have to go higher. It even has a river running through it."

She nodded. "I am backing you. You do what you think's best."

He kissed her again and invited Alan back inside the office. "We're putting our offer at fifteen thousand."

"I'll try."

"Now, for the cattle loan. I have a partner wants a thousand head. He has the money for his. I'd like to have two thousand more head of my own to take up there. Lease for two thousand head is paid for, but I can pay for the rest."

"Whew. I'll ask for that money too."

"I have some assets."

"I can see that. Well, good luck. I should know by tomorrow afternoon. What's that Strip like?"

"Horse heaven. Belly deep in rich bluestem grass and water, but it's isolated as all get out."

"You must hate it, ma'am, being up there with no other women around?"

"No." She shook her head. "I like being with him. We rode down here fine."

"You rode down from Kansas?"

"Yes. We actually came from Ogallala, Nebraska."

Alan shook his head at her remarks. "When I was sixteen, I went to Abilene on my first cattle drive. My butt was so sore when I got back, I went and got an education to become a banker."

Edith laughed. "I guess some take to it easier than others. I thought it was a nice trip riding down here."

"To each their own, I guess," Adams said with a smile.

"That's the truth," Norm said. "I'll be by tomorrow to find out what the verdict is."

"We'll have an answer for you one way or the other. In the meantime, thanks for coming by."

BACK IN THEIR room at the hotel, Norm watched as Edith cut the lining loose in her purse. The sum of her money amounted to nearly eleven thousand dollars.

Norm could hardly believe her savings. "I thought most of the men you saw only had petty cash."

"Remember, I was with Elder. He told me he robbed public officials who could not report the theft, because they'd stolen their money from the public coffers. He found them in southwest Missouri, north Arkansas, and in Kansas. Even some Indians who'd stolen tribal money and had it at home. But he had so little education, he'd bring it to me to count it and be his banker. Each time I did, I hid some of it away and told him he'd taken less than he actually had."

"That was smart."

"I had to be careful. He was the meanest man I ever was with. I think he was beginning to suspect me—that's why he was hitting me when you found us that day."

"What made him suspect?"

"He was always afraid someone was going to rob him. He needed me to help him at first, but eventually he began to distrust me, too." She grinned. "He never found out how right he was."

"Honey, we both struck another path in life, and we help each other. Now, that ill-gotten money will go to help you start over. I hope to make enough money someday we can settle down and lead a normal life."

Seated on the edge of the bed, she hugged him and laughed. "I think today is as normal as it ever will be, living with you, but I love it." She paused. "Do you think they will sell that ranch for that price?"

"I'm certain we will get it. Adams is a good man. He'll do right by us."

"Did you know this man's wife who surrendered the ranch?"

"No, never met her, but her husband was the richest man I ever knew. I suspect that he was heavily borrowed. They said his second wife was a spoiled brat who married him to live high. She spent it."

"I ever die, don't you marry one like that."

"I'm not letting you die, silly. I don't want to break in another one."

"Good." She tackled him, pinning him, laughing, to the bed, and that ended the conversation.

THREE O'CLOCK THE next afternoon, Norm left Edith at the hotel and went to see about the ranch and his loan.

Adams welcomed him in, and he could tell by the man's relaxed face and big smile that he wasn't telling him no.

"They accepted your offer for the price, but the ranch will be secured as part of the cattle loan."

"Good enough. I can pay you eight thousand down and the rest out over five years."

"We can make that work. The place is unlocked. I'm certain you've been there. A Mexican family named Sanchez is staying there at present. His name is Robles, and her name is Modula. They're paid fifteen dollars a month as caretakers."

"Do I get the old rocking chair brand, too?"

"You'll have to transfer it at the court house, but yes."

"That would be a real help to take over an established brand like that."

"I bet it would."

"I'll take Edith out to the ranch tomorrow and show her the place."

Alan looked hard at him. "Think she'll like it?"

Norm shook his head. "I know she will."

"She's a wonderful woman, Mister Thompson. You take care of her."

"I plan to."

"Good. And your new place, too. It once was a helluva ranch."

"I know. I traveled from Montana all the way back here and ended up right where I wanted to be."

"How is it up there in Montana? I heard it's a rough place to be."

"Wonderful seven months. The winters are very hard, though."

"Hell, it gets cold down here, too. Worse than that?"

"Forty below zero?"

Adams gave a shiver. "No. Merciful heaven. How do you survive that?"

"Some don't."

Adams shuddered again. "Too cold for my blood. Anyhow, it's nice to have you back. Hope you make money, and maybe they won't fire me for going into debt over that ranch."

"You loan the old man all that money?"

"No, thank God. It was the bank president, Randall Crane, who did it with an old friend who always came through as a winner."

"Sorry to hear that."

"Hey, I'm riding on your back now. It'll work."

"I'm a pretty stout horse. See you in a few days."

"Can't wait, my friend."

NORM HIGH-TAILED it back to the hotel to tell Edith the news. She grabbed him, and they danced around the room, and she began to sing Beautiful Dreamer and whirl around the room.

He looked down into her sparkling eyes. "Hey, you can sing. You never sang before. You are beautiful. What made you sing?"

"I sang before Elder found me. I never sang again after that until tonight, and you opened my heart when you said we had a ranch and a loan."

"Honey, we have a good start. We can make it work. Sing some more, it lifts me."

"Let me recall more words to them. I think I can still sing hymns. Give me some time."

"Sing anything." He squeezed her tight and swung her around off her feet.

"Put me down. Put me down."

"Never. You are so great I can't believe it. Honey, I am so happy. What can I do more for you?"

She squeezed and kissed him until they collapsed on the bed.

And a great night followed an amazing day for both of them.

CHAPTER No. 6

WHEN NORM AND Edith crossed the last hill that morning, they saw the old twisted and rotten trunks of cottonwood trees that had lined the flowing river for centuries. Dotted nearby were saplings, eternally tapping the mirror-like Pedernales River for their life. Their rented team trotted sharply, and they crossed the bridge, the horses' hooves making a hollow clunk as they pulled the slender wheels of the buggy across. The horses hit the light harness as they went up the white crushed-shell road that wound up the hill. Ahead they saw the rambling white limestone two-story house, with its large hand-hewn beams that he'd heard years ago were cut from virgin oak timber in the Boston Mountains north of Fort Smith, Arkansas. They'd been transported by boat to Louisiana, then up the Red River, and brought southwest by eighteen ox teams pulling eight sets of double wheels per wagon at a snail's pace to this site.

Money was no object to former sea captain Paul Styles. He built this mansion for a yellow woman from New Orleans named La Belle Des Franza. His real wife lived in Galveston, while he lived with La Belle in the great house here and ran the sprawling ranch like a kingdom from the Middle Ages. Like the kings, he was the law, and whatever he said went. There were stories about unfaithful wives of workers who were burned at the stake, or captured Comanche raiders put to death by far worse methods.

But also like a lot of those kings, Styles lost all his money on bad investments. Not only did the banks begin to take an interest, the law, did, too. No way would the Captain and his lover let themselves be deposed by others, so they committed suicide together in the house.

Afterward, the house sat empty for some time, until Farley Mosley made a quarter-million dollars in Abilene, Kansas, selling cattle. He bought the ranch and came to live here with his newly-found, pipe-smoking Arkie wife and her four children. She hated the place. Thought it was too expensive and too far out in the middle of nowhere. Out of her sheer apathy, the ranch was allowed go to ruin. Rumor had it she even let hogs wander through the house. Her children were all too dumb to know better, and when she died, their stepfather, Mosley, had them all committed to the Texas State Lunatic Asylum. But then shortly after his wife's funeral, he bought a teenage girl he adored from her father for three hundred gold *pesos* and married her. She turned out to be a spender—she ran him broke with her high ways, and when he died a few years later, Mosley was in debt to the bank for over a quarter-million dollars.

Norm helped Edith down from the buggy, and she looked around. "It sure needs a lot of work."

"Can't argue with that, but it'll be our home."

"Do you worry that maybe we'll come to the same bad end as the previous two owners?"

"I don't go in much for superstition. People make their own luck, good or bad. We'll do all right."

A small Mexican woman came out onto the porch and greeted Edith with a smile. "I am Modula, *Señora*."

"Glad to meet you. I am Edith. He's Norman."

"You say he is a Mormon? Does he have other wives?"

"No. No. His *name* is Norman, Modula."

Modula laughed. "Oh, I see. I am sorry. The house needs cleaning. I am but one, and my husband works the garden, so we eat."

"Help will be here soon." Norm promised.

Modula led them into the house and gave them a tour. Some pigeons fled from a broken upstairs window flapping their wings like a clapping applause.

"Is it too much to take on?" Norm asked. "You probably wish we'd gotten something in better shape."

"It'll take many hours of labor, but I love it." Edith kissed him softly.

"We can repair the house and clean it. I'll find craftsmen and get more from Mexico. This house will be a great place again.

"So you really don't believe in superstition? You're not afraid that children born here will be crazy?".

Norm laughed. "Even if I believed it, none of Mosley's wife's brood were born here. They were born elsewhere and weren't even his. She brought them here with her. So, no worries, Edith, we're not crazy, nor will our offspring be."

"Well—" She paused. "I hope you're right, because unless you find a different place to live, your first one's going to be born here."

"What?" He was hit broadsided with a board. "When?"

"Oh, May or June."

He looked at her, aghast. Surely, she had to realize what that meant. "I'll be in the Strip."

She nodded. "I know. Don't worry. I'm strong. If God lets him live, I can raise him until you come home."

"I hate for you to be alone."

"I won't be alone. Modula will be here."

The little Mexican woman smiled at them. *"Si, señora."*

She took her hand and gave it a squeeze. "Now, what shall we do first?"

"Go back to town and get married," Norm said. "For real this time. Hire some help, get some supplies, and make this damn place a real ranch. Get some shotgun shells, too. I'm sure as hell not sharing my house with any damn pigeons."

He met Modula's husband, Robles, too. A kind man with calloused hands who acted pleased that someone had at last come to bring this place back to its former beauty.

Modula fixed them some lunch, and they rode back to town. Edith had a list, and he left her at the mercantile to fill their needs. He went by the stock yards, but saw none of his new hands there yet. So he went looking for artisans, instead. He ended up speaking with two Mexican men.

"Are there any craftsmen here?"

"What do you need, *señor?*"

He looked them both over. "Some rock masons. Carpenter, repair men." .

"*Si,* my brother and I can get them. Where do you need them?"

"Rocking Chair Ranch. I'm the new owner, and it needs remodeled."

The man's eyes grew wide. "That place? It has a history, you know, *señor.*"

"I know all about it. But I'm gonna do what I can to change it for the better. We have to rent some wagons to haul sand and cement for mortar. It will take several bundles of cedar shingles and nails."

The man nodded.

"See to that. The workers will need to replace the broken glass and get putty to seal them when they replace them."

His friend nodded. "In three days, we will be there with ten men and handle all of it for you, *señor.* They will work. It is good that someone is there to care for the ranch as it should be."

"With your help. Oh, and what is your name?"

"We are the Reynalles brothers. He is Gus, and I am Leon."

"I'm Norman Thompson. See you then."

He went to the store where he found Edith on the porch with a man in worker overalls.

"Darling, this is Jim Lawrence. I hired him to do some hauling. He also replaces glass windows. He's taking our supplies up and will stay to fix the broken glass."

"Good. I hired a pair of brothers who will be coming to repair the roof, and the masonry. They're bringing carpenters, too."

"That will be accomplishing a lot," she said.

"I want your house fixed up like new in no time."

"Thank you, darling." She kissed him. "Jim here is going up there with his load tomorrow and will stay until he has all the windows fixed. He's taking up all the food and items you wanted ordered for the ranch too."

Jim nodded. "And I'd sure appreciate any work like hauling or repairs you need done after that."

"I think we can use you a lot starting out."

"Oh." Edith put a hand to her chest. "What time is it?"

Jim looked inside at the store clock. "Three thirty."

She took Norm's hand. "You have thirty minutes to get me to the Baptist Church. Parson Holmes is marrying us then."

"You work fast, dear. But heavens, I'm fine with that. Jim, we better run."

"Yes, you better do that! Nice to meet you two, sir. And good luck."

The wedding was simple and over quickly, but they had the most important part—the marriage certificate—signed and in their hands. Then they went to the hotel for their honeymoon.

Later, in the hotel room, she wore a duster and stood at the second story window to watch the street traffic. "I worried something bad would happen, like the last time I got married."

"Really, sometimes you do get superstitious on me."

"I have reason to be. You never had such a bad experience happen to you, while mine went on for almost two years, until you came and saved me."

"Darling, it won't ever happen to you again. I promise."

They were in love's arms again.

Later that evening, he lay next to her in bed, his head propped up on one arm. "Tell me one thing. Why did you change your mind about marriage so suddenly?"

"You said we needed to get married. I met the preacher in the store. He was friendly, and with the baby coming, I thought we better get to it while we had the opportunity." She paused, and he saw worry cross her brow. "So many women can't carry one to full term. I plan to have this one."

"Honey, so do I."

"You won't leave me, if I lose it?"

"I won't leave you, period."

In four weeks, they had a house-warming fandango in the huge, newly remodeled *casa,* and everyone they knew or met was invited. Norm bought a corn-fat steer and two fat hogs to barbecue. They borrowed every table and bench they could from nearby churches and schools.

The entire crew of workers and their wives cooked food for twenty-four hours. They had music, and he even got his wife to sing. The whole countryside came to the christening of his new house and chatted and sighed about the lovely building resurrected from the decay of the old one.

The minister who married them attended and blessed it.

The deputy for Bexar County told him on the side, "You sure need to count your horses on a regular basis around here, 'cause they're stealing lots of them."

"Well, when I get some horses bought, I will damn sure count them."

"You have any trouble, Mister Thompson, you kin sure call on me, sir. Henry Sims."

"Thanks, Henry. I learn anything suspicious, I'll report it to you."

Next day, Cur Taylor, one of the men he'd signed on as his crew, rode in on a spent horse to meet them at the front porch and dismounted.

The bowlegged short cowboy spoke right up. "How you doing, Norm? Man, Missus Thompson, you two sure moved up from them packhorses to this fancy place fast. Folks told me back in town it was a mansion. Looks more like a castle to me. You need some hands for this place?"

"Guess I could use some good ones. You available?"

He removed his hat and craned his head around. "Oh hell, all this place needs is some mother cows. Yeah, I'd work for you, and I'd damn sure work for the brand."

"Have a seat over on this bench, and let's talk about it. I'll need some mother cows, for sure. But I am going to need lots of help gathering three thousand head of yearlings this winter to take north in the spring to the Cherokee Strip."

"Wow, you're going big as this house, huh?" Cur twirled his sweat-stained felt hat on his hand between his knees. "Would you seriously consider me for the foreman job?"

"Yeah, When do you want to start?"

"Two days."

"What've you got in mind?"

He blushed. "Aw, I've got a girl, see? She's a sweet Mexican gal, lives down there on the Gonzales River. I want to marry her."

"You plan to marry her?"

"Yeah."

"Edith. Come out here." He grinned at Cur. "Hold tight."

"What is it?" Edith came out the door, bringing glasses of cool tea to them on a tray.

"Cur wants to marry a woman in town. Can't they do that out here?"

"Why, heavens, yes. Is he coming to work for you?"

"He's going to be a foreman here or the Strip. But that's future. He needs a place to get married."

"Who is the lucky girl?"

"Name's Margarita Valdez. Got two sweet kids."

"Oh, Cur, we can fix up one of the *jacals* for you to live in—four huh?"

"Yes."

"Could we do it Saturday? The marriage?"

"Sure. I'll get a wagon and move her into the *jacal* if it's all right?"

Cur seemed shaken from all things happening around him so fast. But they all were soon set for it to take place. Cur brought Margarita and the two small children out with all their things in Jim's wagon.

At his first meeting with her, Norm wondered if she'd wait to have the baby in her belly until after the marriage. But his wife took charge, and the pretty girl in her teens acted very excited about a house of her own and the pending marriage.

Later they talked privately about the pairing.

"She loves him." Norm stretched out his legs. "Cur told me she had been in slavery, too. He took her away from it to marry her."

"I believe she'll make him a wife... like another sad girl did for you."

"It worked out for me, didn't it?" He hugged and kissed her. "I bought a dozen horses to start a *remuda*. I get delivery next Friday. But I have our horses and the packhorses to ride. Maybe a horse thief will steal that bay."

"You can always hope."

They both laughed.

Two days before the wedding, they went over their plans.

"The beef I ordered is coming in this morning. The workers are ready for another celebration."

Norm looked her over carefully. "And how do you feel?"

"Fine. I'm not doing anything stressful or real physical."

"I invited Alan Adams to bring his lady along tomorrow night. They missed the housewarming. He said he'd come."

"He married?"

"No, but I don't need to know the rest."

"I'm amused about the two of you and how your two lives split. The summer after the first drive, you learned how to swim, and he came home and trained to be banker, so he didn't have to go again."

Half the crew that the Reynalles brothers brought out to work had stayed on to remodel the *jacals* where the ranch hands with families stayed, the bunkhouse for the single workers and cowboys, and the mess hall. Several of them had chosen to become ranch staff, and their wives joined the big house staff. As a result, they had many small, dark-eyed children who came to work with their mothers at the big house.

Of course, Edith knew all their names and spoiled them rotten.

With the wedding at hand, some of Edith's crew sewed the bride a new dress. Edith bought the material, thread, needles, and the rest. The end result was beautiful, and made young Margarita cry. Meanwhile, the men built the fires for the cooking and worked hard at all of it. The workers thanked him often for their jobs and the home-like society they were building.

Cur and Margarita's wedding was performed by Father Farley, and the food and fun began. While the celebration was in full swing, a rancher named Marty Cole separated Norm from the rest of the party.

Cole was a short, mustached man in his forties, known to be a fair and honest man. His brand was the MC Bar. "They say you need yearlings?"

"I plan to buy some when the loans are final."

"What will you pay for them?"

"Real yearlings are, right now, fifteen bucks, because I'll need to feed them this winter."

"If I feed them and road-brand them, then deliver them when you're ready to go north, what are they worth then?"

"Twenty bucks. Steers only."

Cole nodded.

"How many do you have?"

"I can guarantee you five hundred head."

"That sounds good, Cole. What do I need to do to make our trade?"

"Advance me a thousand dollars. I need to make a place payment before that happens."

"Cattle mortgaged?"

"No, only the land. I don't want them mortgaged and have them tell me when to sell or not."

"I'll have my lawyer draw up a contract. When do you need the money?"

"Monday."

"I can arrange that. I'll meet you at ten a.m. at the lawyer Rob Sneed's office. You know the place?"

"Sure do. Rob's a good man. This helps me and helps you at the same time. I worried how I was going to make that payment. I'll tell my wife." They shook hands on it, and Cole walked away.

"You make a deal?" Edith asked him later, before the party was over.

"Five hundred head delivered next spring, rebranded. Twenty dollars a head, and he'll deliver them. He needs a thousand dollars now and the rest of the money next spring at delivery."

"That's a big chunk of the cattle that you needed already."

"You bet it is. And I'm pretty sure Cole won't short me or bring any less than healthy animals, either."

"So, all you need are twenty-five hundred more." She kissed his cheek and smiled at the laughter and talk going on around them. "The party is going well. I'm meeting lots of your friends."

"Strange to me how people that never gave me a look back when I was a poor kid living south of Kerrville are now my best friends."

"They want everyone to know they're friends of the new owner of the Rocking Chair."

"That's about right."

She gave him a beguiling smile. "Maybe we should dance?"

"I don't know if I remember how. I've been out of the center of real people so long I forgot."

"You'll remember."

He put one hand on her belly. "Will the baby mind?"

"Not at all. He'll be fine."

"It might be a girl."

She frowned at him hard. "No, it'll be a boy."

"You're sure?"

She hugged him. "I'm sure. And he'll be just like his father."

"I pity you. I was a hell-raiser as a kid." She laughed as Norm continued, "I am going to ride around the ranch some the next couple of days and look at things. I've never seen it all, and I need to know it."

"Take someone along. This house and ranch say you are worth something, and if there are outlaws around, they might think you have money. You can't be too careful"

"Yes, ma'am."

"Two are better than one."

He left her to go and find Rowdy Kimmel, another of his hired men. The big cowboy was drinking from a mug of beer at the keg with some men from town that had been invited out for the wedding party.

"What's up, boss man?"

"Let's saddle up about sunup and look some at this place. There are parts I haven't seen yet."

"What horse you want your saddle on?"

"Tell Rico, the Montana horse."

"No problem. I'll be at the horse barn area whenever you are ready."

"Come have breakfast at six thirty in the kitchen. I'll tell them you're coming so they'll have a plate waiting for you."

"I appreciate the invite."

"No big deal. How are you guys?" he asked the others standing there.

"Fine." A taller man scuffed his boot on the dirt. "We were just about to ask you about your cattle needs. Cole said he sold you some yearlings for spring delivery. Last year I sent all my big steers north to Kansas, and you know, expenses go on. How many could you buy—yearlings, right?"

"Yep. And I only buy steers. No bawling calves. How many would you be willing to part with?"

"Three-four hundred head. I'm Sammy Daniels, by the way. S D Ranch."

The two shook hands. "Nice to meet you, Sammy. I'd pay fifteen bucks a head now, or rebranded and delivered next spring for twenty."

"If I promised you four hundred head in the spring, could I get a five hundred dollar advance?"

"I want stubby-horned steers, not just weaned ones. I mean yearlings."

"I savvy that." Daniels nodded. "I'll have them to suit you."

"We can sign papers on them on Tuesday for the deal."

A second man shook his hand. "Joel McKinney. If I brought you sixty head here now, you'd pay me fifteen a head?"

Norm nodded. "Sure would. When you bringing them?"

"I'd have them gathered and here by next Friday."

"I'll pay you on acceptance."

"I'm not as big as these other guys, and I don't have to tell you that any kind of money has been short around here ever since the damn war. That's a fair market, and I appreciate it."

Norm clapped him on the back. "Hell, we were all poor back then."

They all laughed. When the two ranchers took their beer mugs and went to find their better halves, Rowdy nudged him. "Hey, this steer buying is going pretty good already."

"Yeah, I'm pleased. We'll have close to a third of our cattle bought in the next week or two."

"I bet you get more when the word gets out. I'd never thought so many would sell those lighter cattle—hell, in another year they'd be big enough to ship north and get full price for."

"Money, Rowdy. They all need money now."

"You're right. Costs money to live, don't it?"

"Or to fix up a rundown *hacienda* and stock it."

"Cur's had us checking things and driving the other brands off our land. The bank's hired round-up crew. Cur and I figure we have a hundred cows and several crossbred bulls we need to cut, plus the calves that need branded."

"Good. We have a start, anyhow, and they're ours by the terms of my purchase. After frost and the screw worms are gone, we'll have a big round-up and get that straight."

"We also saw some running-iron branded calves with different brands than their momma's."

"The deputy sheriff assigned up here says they steal horses, too."

Rowdy shook his head. "I met that dumb pecker-wood. He don't impress me at all."

"I'm the same way. He ain't very smart, but he is the law. I haven't seen Cur. You see him, tell him he should join us for breakfast. He don't need to ride with us. We're just looking tomorrow."

"I can tell you now that he'll be there. He's kinda staying close to his bride these days. You know, with her about to spring."

Norm smiled. His foreman was doing his job fine—but his little bride was getting close, and she was his new toy. He knew all about new toys—he had one, too. "See you at breakfast."

"Word's out," Edith said, joining him. "You're buying cattle at a fair price."

"Rancher's wives talking about it?"

"Oh, yes. I bet they come from El Paso to sell you cattle."

He laughed and hugged her shoulder. Whoever would have guessed about her tent in Ogallala? She looked the full part a rancher's wife and acted the same at that. Plus, she finally seemed completely happy. That amazed him the most.

After the wedding event was over, Jim and some ranch help with borrowed teams and wagons would spend all night again cleaning up and returning the borrowed tables and benches to the church and school.

"You'd best make your own tables and benches if you're gonna have weddings out here this often," one of the men said with a laugh.

"You know, that's not a half bad idea." Norm scratched his chin. "We'll see to that once everything else is done."

They went to bed late. The party was a big success, and everyone had fun.

"Damn you, Norman Thompson. If I'd known you were coming to rescue me from hell back then, I'd sure acted better when you first came hat in hand to my tent. But I believed you, and you've done everything you promised. Food and a dry place, you said. Here, we live in a palace and have a rich life."

She rolled over and kissed the fire out of him.

Thank you, God—one more time.

CHAPTER No. 7

EDITH AND MODULA served a big breakfast to Norm, Cur, Rowdy, and Chet while they sipped fresh hot coffee and discussed the ranch's future.

"Last night, I bought near a thousand yearlings," Norm said. "I only have to pay fifteen for sixty head coming in a week. The rest will be re-branded and delivered next spring. We talked about our own cattle here and working them after frost when the screw worm flies are gone."

Cur agreed. "Rowdy and I have been building a herd book. We could use some more Shorthorn or Hereford bulls to replace the crossbred ones they left 'cause they're so damn wild. I plan to team rope and cut them at roundup if you can afford British bulls to replace them."

"That's a good idea. I'll find the bulls, or you can find me some good ones."

"I'll put the word out," Cur said.

Edith asked him, "How's your wife feeling?"

He took the large platter of food from her, but grinned and shook his head. "I'm still full from last night's fandango. She's feeling great but very close—I check on her all the time."

"Need me to take some off that plate?" Edith asked him.

"No, ma'am, it looks so good, I'll find room to stuff it in."

She put her hand on his shoulder and laughed. "You cowboys always do."

"It's easy when the food's good, and you have wonderful women who bring it to you. Right, Rowdy?"

"Sure thing. These two ladies can handle it for me, as well."

Cur cradled a warm coffee cup in his hands. "At this rate, they're gonna make me fat."

"Fat? No way. Not the way you run around." Edith shook her head, went back for more plates of food.

After breakfast, Norm and Rowdy rode out on their inspection tour. Norm thought Montana might buck. He hadn't ridden him in a while, but he never gave him a chance to try. The cowpony single-footed sideways up the farm road, making two faint sets of tracks in the grass.

At last with Norm's horse settled, Rowdy asked him where he found such a sweet lady to marry.

"Her last man was beating her up in an alley. I saw it. Made me mad. I knocked him on his ass, then found out he was a wanted outlaw. After that, I went and found her again and offered to take her along with me. She came."

"You're a lucky man, Norm. You fell into a pile of shit and came out smelling like a rose. Up in Kansas one time, a guy was beating a woman with a stick in the street. I got off my horse and took his stick away and went to beating him. Next thing, she was on my back screaming, 'Don't hit my husband!' So, you can't win them all."

"I'd still stop and try to make them quit."

"Oh, I wasn't soured on my effort. Just didn't turn out like I planned. I'd still stop and try."

They spooked up some Rocking Chair Ranch branded cows with their large unbranded calves. The live water in many branches and gullies was a good sign, but it had been a wet year. Rowdy didn't think they usually had this much water this late, and the ranch would probably need more tanks and windmills to keep the cattle spread out.

As they approached a makeshift campsite, a bearded man in gray underwear and dirt-stained pants ducked out from under the canvas flap of a tent. His hand was on his gun butt like he aimed to draw it.

Norm beat him to the punch, already had his gun drawn. "Get your damn hand off that gun, mister."

For a second, he wasn't sure this worthless outfit would do as ordered. In the end, though, the intruder spread his hands, palms out.

Norm angled his head toward Rowdy. "Watch yourself."

"Hell, yes, I will."

He turned back to the squatter. "My name's Norman Thompson. This is my land. You can't homestead it."

"This is Texas land, and I can stake it. You big ranch owners don't own all of it."

"Friend, you better plan to load up, or I'll have the sheriff move you."

"Yeah, yeah. You bastards bought off the law, too, didn't you?"

Norm saw a slender girl hanging back in the shade. "That your wife?"

"Hell, yes."

She shook her head over. "I ain't his wife, mister. He kidnapped me months ago. Help me."

"Shut your damn mouth, woman, or I'll bust it for you—"

Norm cut him off. "Rowdy, keep your gun on him. You ain't busting anyone in the mouth. Young lady come out here and tell me the whole story."

Norm and Rowdy both dismounted. Rowdy drew his pistol and pushed the man backward. "Come out here, girl."

"About two months ago, he caught me—"

"Shut your mouth! She's my wife, and she ain't none of your damn business."

By then, the woman was in tears, eyes filled with fear. "I ain't his wife. He raped me and took me away. He'll beat me after telling you this—"

Rowdy shook his head. "Oh, no, he won't, ma'am."

Norm jerked his chin at her. "What's your name?"

"Mattie Cornwall."

"Where you from?"

"Way east of Dallas. Purty Wells."

He turned to the squatter. "What's your name, mister?"

"Clayton Boles."

She shook her head. "Tha ain't his name."

Rowdy stepped forward and disarmed the man. "Then who is he?"

"Gerald Roberts, and he's wanted for murders and robbery."

"Damn yellow bitch! When this is over, I'm going to beat your ass raw."

Norm cocked his fist. "Shut up."

"That's what she is. Just a yellar whore. She ain't telling yah the truth."

Norm shook his head. "Her ancestry don't count. You're going to jail, and we'll let the law decide your fate, whatever your name is."

They let her gather her things. She had damn little of anything worth hauling, and their horses were thin. Roberts had used two colts for pack-horses, and they looked spent. Norm just turned them out. They tied Roberts up with his hands behind his back, then they brought the pair back to the ranch.

With a puzzled look written on her face, Edith came out to meet them.

"Edith, meet Mattie. This guy kidnapped her a while back and held her prisoner. She says he's wanted. The law can decide that part. I'm going to send Rowdy and another hand to deliver him to the deputy."

"You're a mess. Still finding outlaws." Edith kissed him on the cheek and shook her head in disbelief. "Come along, Mattie. We can find you a hot bath and some clothes to wear until we find some your size. You can tell me all about your ordeal."

Rowdy and Burt Randle, another ranch hand, took the prisoner to town the next morning. Norm gave them expense money for meals and a room at the hotel for the night, and told them to watch him close.

"Damn sure we will." Rowdy patted the Colt strapped to his leg. "I don't trust that feller as far as I could kick him."

After they'd taken Roberts away, Edith told him that Mattie had confessed that her grandmother was half-black. In Texas, even with slavery over and done with, people referred to anyone with black blood as yellow.

Norm shook his head. The girl deserved better than that damn outlaw.

"Don't worry, dear, she'll be a pretty woman someday. She was starved, mistreated like I was, beaten all the time."

"How old is she?"

"Thirteen or fourteen is all. I just hope she isn't with child."

"That'd make a bad situation worse."

She sighed. "You see much of the ranch?"

"No, I have lots more to see yet. But we do have several cattle they missed."

"Two men were here to sell you their yearlings while you were gone. A man named Cobb and one named Jensen. They'll be back."

"Good. I'll find them." He gave her a hug.

When Rowdy and Randle came back the next day, they told Norm that there was, indeed, a reward out on Roberts. There might be other rewards as well, but two hundred was the only one for sure so far. They also brought the squatter's horse back with him and turned him out in the corral.

"Try again to take that tour tomorrow?" Rowdy asked.

"Sure. Breakfast early. Invite Cur to come with us."

Norm went back in to the house. He was a long way from a payday. Maybe a year and a half. That much time would strain his resources, and his wife would need help there, too, preparing for the new baby. Oh well, somehow, he'd make it. Somehow. There must be hundreds of wanted outlaws out there. He'd run across a slew of them in the last few months, and the rewards had all helped. Maybe he could find a few more.

Edith looked up from her sewing. "Going back out tomorrow?"

"Yes. I just finished talking to Rowdy. He doesn't think there are any more squatters, but with the sections we own, there could be more. Maybe concealed better than this man was. How's our girl doing?"

"I think she's somewhere between relief and shock. She's realizing she's free, and no one will harm her here. Now, the question remaining is to find out if she's pregnant. She *has* had periods. But only the good Lord can know. My heavens, why did he kidnap such a young woman?"

"Easier to make them submit."

"I can see that." Edith shook her head. "It's horrible, though. At least she will be safe here, though."

"You tell her your story?"

"Yes. She understood we'd shared lots of the same problems."

"You feeling all right?"

"Oh, I'm fine. I don't even know there's a baby growing inside of me. Let's go to bed. You have to get up early."

"You can sleep in."

Her frown looked serious. "I want to be around when you are here. I am proud to be your wife, and I know we will be separated a long time when you are up in the Strip."

"Does that bother you?"

"Not as long as you're careful and come back here to me."

"Wild horses couldn't keep me from doing that."

T HE NEXT DAY, he and Rowdy rode past the tarp Roberts had strung between the cottonwood trees. He'd send some of the younger boys up to take it down and bring anything of value back to the ranch.

At a creek crossing, Rowdy got off his horse and studied the ground. "Hey, Norm, come look at these tracks. There was a barefoot horse come through since we were here yesterday. It was packing a rider, too, I'll bet. And it wasn't one of those colts we turned loose."

Norman examined the track for himself. "You been seeing tracks like that anywhere else?"

"I thought maybe it was an old ranch horse they turned out. But the horses the boys ride are all shod. This one's packing a rider. The imprints are deep in the soft ground." He pointed. "See, his whole frog shows here."

Norm knelt down on the bank. "It may be another squatter come by to see them and found them gone."

"Whoever it was, his horse must be crooked-footed on his right front leg."

"We'll keep our eyes open. My back itches a lot since I came back from Montana. I never told Edith about it, because I didn't want both of us wondering about it."

"I'll keep my eye out, boss."

"Hey, good observation. You've got sharp eyes. I wouldn't have noticed it."

They covered lots of country and found more Rocking Chair cattle and their unbranded calves. They also came upon up a small herd of yearlings with no brands at all, a mix of heifers and bull calves that hadn't been cut.

Rowdy adjusted the brim of his hat. "We'll have lots of work this fall working all the stock they left behind."

They were riding through some cedar-crowded hill country, and he saw the forest of standing fence posts. On the far side, waving, stirrup-high grass spilled out like an ocean.

"I bet this is where the water will be short for the stock. It may take windmills to pump it up for them here."

Rowdy shook his head. "You're the cow man. I'd never thought about the reason for such a great meadow being less grazed was water."

"You found tracks I'd never bothered with before. Everyone does what they do best. We work together as a team." Norm looked into the distance, shading his eyes with one hand. "Hey, look. There are a few more cattle up north of us."

Rowdy whistled. "One of them's a giant. Damn, I never saw a bull that big in my life."

"Hell, he must weigh a ton. He's a chocolate red color longhorn cross, and he's sixteen-hands at the shoulder, I'd say from here. Don't stir him—he'll take some real ropers to ever get him."

They found no more tracks from the barefoot horse, but one was enough to make Norm wonder. Surely no one had ridden down here after him from Montana, right?

Then he remembered the lone horseman he'd seen trailing him and Edith on their way here. Damn. He couldn't possibly answer that question and be satisfied with his own answer.

CHAPTER No. 8

THE NEXT DAY, Norm and Rowdy rode further west, where they found more ranch cattle and un-branded calves. It was a hotter day, but they covered lots of ground. This was the same kind of country as they found up north, running from live oak and cedar hills to miles of rolling grass and dry hillsides with prickly pear patches. Quail blasted out of bushy places. Squirrels bounded off chattering, and jackrabbits bounded away as if they had springs for legs. Some trophy bucks melted into the vegetation.

They were on a small creek with a good running flow. Norm dismounted to water his horse, and his nostrils caught the hint of oak smoke on the air.

"You catch the smell?"

"Just as you said that. They can't be far away."

"More squatters, you think?"

"Or rustlers, maybe?" Rowdy shook his head that he had no answer. "Let's hobble the horses and try to sneak up on them."

"Good idea. Get your rifle." Norm jerked his own out of the scabbard. He cracked the lever, and when satisfied a brass cartridge was in the chamber, closed it back.

They hobbled their ponies. Their girths loosened, they set out up the creek toward the source of the smoke. Lots of old gnarled cottonwoods lined the bank and a hundred years of cattle tracks—maybe even once used by buffalo—cut into the earth.

Norm finally caught sight of the fire, then heard some calves bawling. A man with a branding iron pressed a hot brand down on one of them. Other struggling and complaining calves were tied up on the ground awaiting their turn.

"Only two of them?" Rowdy whispered.

He nodded. "They're packing guns, too. They'll fight before being caught rustling, I'll bet."

"Order them to throw up their hands." Rowdy pointed. "I'm going to use that tree to steady my rifle. If they want to fight, I'll shoot them. We're out of easy pistol range."

Norm nodded, his rifle stock snugged in against his shoulder. "Get your hands in the air or die!"

"Who in the fuck are you?" The rustler threw the branding iron aside and went for his pistol. Norm shot him in the shoulder, and he dropped the gun, screaming. "You shot me."

Rowdy's first shot didn't hit the second one. The rustler turned and ran, but the next shot knocked the man off his feet. He sprawled on the ground screaming, too.

"Watch it!" Still crouched, Norm kept the rifle barrel on the outlaws. "They may still try something."

"Oh, I've got my six-gun ready, boss. Sons of bitches. Cur and I never saw any sign of rustling fires like this, but we have seen some brands that don't belong. And XYZ was one of them."

Norm stood over the first one. He looked a lot younger than he'd first thought. "What's your name?"

The rustler looked at the blood seeping out from under the hand he'd clamped on his shoulder. He didn't answer, so Norm kicked him in the side, and he screamed.

"Luke Meaders. You've killed me, you sumbitch."

"That's what rustlers get—killed. Your pa know you're here?"

"Hell, no. You crazy?"

"How many of my calves have you brand?"

"Screw you."

"You want kicked again?"

"Maybe a dozen."

"Right." Norm didn't believe that for a second. He jacked the lever on the rifle again. "Tell me, or you die right now.

"Thirty! Thirty or so! Please, mister, get a doctor for us."

"You two won't need a doctor where you're going."

The youth's face paled. "What'cha mean?"

"Rowdy and I handle our own rustling cases. Start saying your prayers to your lord and savior, boy, 'cause in a short while you'll be with him. Or with the devil in hell."

The boy's blue eyes flew open. "You going to hang us?"

He grinned. "And we won't be long doing it."

"Please, sir, don't do that...."

Rowdy scowled as he tromped back over from the other young rustler. "That's Buck Meaders over there, and he's been hit twice. I'll go get the lariats."

"Grim job, but they knew what they were doing and what they'd get if they were caught. I'll untie the calves and let 'em go. Their bawling is almost as bad as these rustlers."

Norman went for the rustlers' saddled horses standing hipshot in the shade. He led them back as Rowdy made the nooses. With that done, they pushed the screaming Luke down on his belly and tied his bloody hands behind his back. Then they did the same to his nearly unconscious brother.

"You can't just hang us!" Luke screamed. "Please!"

They put the two on horseback and led them to a thick tree branch he wanted them under. Norm took the XYZ branding iron and tied it around Luke's neck with some string. When eventually someone found the pair, the finders would know their offenses.

Buck about fell off his horse, but Norm stopped his fall and set him back up. He held him and the horses while Rowdy mounted up, rode over, and pulled the knot around the kid's neck and tightened the noose. Then he did the same thing to Luke's noose. The boy was weeping now, but he knew he was done for and had stopped pleading for his life.

Norm tied up the reins on the horses' necks, then stepped aside. With a shout, Rowdy smacked both horses on their butts, and they bolted away.

The lariats yanked tight, and both rustlers fell to their death.

The loud snap of neck bones being severed satisfied Norman. He hated botched hangings where the condemned shit their pants and danced until they strangled to death. The bodies twisted around on the ends of the ropes, and the branding iron still decorated his chest. Their horses would wander home.

Bad as he hated it, this had been cold, hard justice.

The execution had apparently torn up Rowdy, as well. "I wish we hadn't had to do that."

"No thing for it, my friend." About then, Norm remembered the sealed half-pint of whiskey he kept in his saddlebags. "Hold up."

He took the bottle out. Using his jackknife, he cut the seal and uncorked it. He handed it over. After a swallow and a shiver, Rowdy handed it back. Norm took a big slug himself and passed it over so his man could finish it off.

When he was done, Rowdy reared back and threw it as far as he could. The sound of it smashing on a rock echoed across the hills. "Sorry, boss. At times, this job gets real tough."

"Those types don't quit rustling unless you string 'em up, Rowdy. We may get some bad talk from it, but we can't let every Tom, Dick, and Jonah rustle our cattle. We did what was necessary. Stopped it, and now."

"Been one helluva day, bossman." Rowdy sighed. "And I know I may have to do it myself someday. I won't let you down."

"I know you won't. I'll tell you what. If Cur can ever leave his new doll, I want him to go north next spring. I want you to be foreman here while I'm gone. You'll be in charge."

That brought the younger man's head around. "Why, thanks. I'd be proud to do it. It'd be an honor."

"Good." Norm nodded. " Now let's head home. I've seen enough for today."

CHAPTER No. 9

THE MASKED RIDERS came around midnight, three nights later. Edith heard them and woke him up. Norm saw the glare of torchlight flashing on the bedroom window glass.

"Who are they?"

"Just stay here. I'll go face them."

"No, Norm. Don't."

"I have to or they'll fire the whole place."

"What if they kill you?'

"I won't let them."

Pulling on his clothes, he strapped on his gun belt and opened the window. "I hear you. I'm coming down to talk."

He was met with a storm of cussing and yelling.

"My wife and several families are here on the ranch. Watch your damn language, or else."

There was some low, sinister laughter, but the swearing stopped. After a short kiss, he rambled down the stairs, walked out on the porch, and faced the torchlight.

Had he given his crew enough time to surround them? He hoped so.

"Now, what's this all about?"

"You son of a bitch, you and your men lynched my boys for trespassing over on Collard Creek."

"You must be Mister Meaders. Your boys weren't trespassing. They were rustling and branding calves on my property, by their own admission. They'd been doing that on a regular basis, too. There are as many as three-dozen calves sucking on my cows wearing your brand. You brand any of them yourself?"

"Hell, no, And they weren't rustling, either."

"Yes, sir, they were. Your boys were caught red-handed rustling my livestock, and they've been doing so for months. They got exactly what they deserved, and you know it."

"I'm going to—"

"You better be real careful with what you say next, Meaders. Right now, I have fifteen men with loaded rifles surrounding you and your little posse. One wrong move, and you'll be able to ask your sons if they were rustling or not in person."

Out of the darkness, a dozen-lever action rifles clacked noisily. The nightriders all sat upright in their saddles, and looked around.

"That's right. You heard 'em. Now, turn around and go home, and you tell anyone you want that Rocking Chair'll lynch any rustlers caught stealing our cattle."

Meaders just glared at him. "This ain't over, Thompson."

Norm drew his own pistol now. "Oh, yes, it is. Now, dammit—*git!*"

With slow, sullen movements, Meaders and his men backed away from the house, turned their horses around and filed away into the night.

Rowdy and Cur both climbed the porch steps as Norm watched them go.

Cur was first to speak. "Did that old man really think he was going to come over here and hang you?"

"Probably not, but I don't trust him. From now on, any of our men riding out should be in pairs."

Rowdy spat. "With their rifles loaded."

"Amen to that." Norm nodded. He knew that another mess had been added to his life. Better go see about Edith—she wasn't going to like this.

BACK IN THE house, Edith, Modula, and Mattie cried fearful tears in the living room. Norm shook his head and spoke softly to them. "Ladies, stop crying. No one was hurt here. This, too, will pass. Nothing will come of it."

"Norman!" Edith shook her head. "They came to kill you."

"No, they came here to try to scare us into leaving. Don't worry. I won't put up with threats or be run off. When I was a boy, the Comanche came by our ranch on a raid. We met them with gunfire, and they never came to our place again. You can't meet threats with weakness. This, too, will pass, my love."

The three women nodded, and Edith joined him. "Being woken by men with torches is scary."

"Yes, I understand. But words can't hurt you. You can't hold a gun when you've got a torch in one hand and the reins to your horse in the other. You know that." He hugged his wife and kissed her. "Let's all go back to bed."

He'd need to leave a ready team of men on the ranch while he was gone to the Strip to protect his investment—and his lovely wife, as well. Rowdy could do the job, but he'd need a good group of tough hands to back him up. They'd talk more about it over the winter. One more thing to worry about. And the Meadors boys wouldn't be the last rustlers they'd have to deal with, either.

Edith felt better about the matter in the morning. Her housekeeper, Modula, and the girl, Mattie, acted like they understood the episode was over and there was nothing to worry about. He was finishing his breakfast of pancakes and homemade syrup when his two right-hand men arrived.

Modula poured them coffee while Norm got down to business.

"Well, do we need a sentry system here?"

"I think we could do that." Cur nodded. "Rowdy and I talked about making a nightly guard duty schedule. We need a schoolhouse warning bell like they had on a ranch I worked on down south. That would make our folks roll out in time to defend the place."

"Then we need to find one."

Rowdy agreed. "I'll go down to Kerrville and find a used one."

"Good idea. Edith will give you some expense money. Take a packhorse, though, that'd be pretty heavy in your lap."

Rowdy laughed at the notion. "I'll do that. Thanks."

After the meeting, Norm and Edith went over their budget—the cost for all their help, other expenses, and how long they had to wait for any real income. It was a big job, but they got a handle on it.

"We'll have to borrow some money to operate through next year. I expected that, but we should have the ability pay it all back when it's over."

"Will they loan you more money?"

"They'll have to, or herd the cattle on the Strip themselves."

"You promised me it would be a poker game." She swung on his neck. "It will be close to one, I bet."

He kissed her. "We may have a hundred yearlings of our own. We'll know at roundup in six weeks. I may ask the boys to take a cut in pay until we get through. We'll pay them the balance after we sell the steers."

"Will this rustling deal stop your cattle buying?"

He shook his head. "No one in the ranch business likes rustlers. They'd rustled over thirty of our calves. To some ranchers that loss would ruin them financially. Meaders won't get much more than family support."

"Well, my love, I really like this new life, but I could live in a cow camp with you and never complain."

He smiled at her. "I may need to take you up on that before this is over."

"No. You'll figure it all out."

"I appreciate you and your support." He nodded toward Mattie, who was helping Modula in the kitchen. "That girl is becoming like a daughter to you, isn't she?"

"Yes. She'll recover and make something out of herself. And she isn't carrying his baby."

"Well, that, at least, is good news."

It would give Edith something to focus on, besides the threat from the Meaders family. He wondered what they'd try next. People like that wouldn't just give up. Norm and his men would have to be ready to repel any attack. But damned if he'd be run off, and if that man wanted war, he'd get it and something else besides.

Out in the shop, Cur and Rowdy were building a chuckwagon with some of the other hands. Jim had found them a stout army ambulance, and the ranch's own handy carpenters had gone all over it. They'd built a cupboard, sewed a new canvas cover, and made a shade off the back to so the men could have a dry place to eat on rainy days. It had eight poles to be anchored down and support the tent-like structure.

Things were moving along well. Norm was pleased with the progress being made restoring the place to a working ranch.

The old pens had been patched many times before, and he'd made a decision to rebuild them and make them larger. Three men were cutting cedars for posts and rails. Meanwhile, horses were being worked and the sorry ones culled. Rowdy told him the bay horse they'd taken from the outlaws, despite his evil disposition, was a natural cutting horse, and that they'd use him as such.

"Good luck dodging his orneriness." Norm laughed. "My leg still remembers when I didn't move fast enough."

Cur reported that there were several mustangs on the ranch that might be good prospects for their *remuda*. He'd been scouting them, and he felt there were several horses that would make good mounts.

The next morning, Norm and Cur set out early for where the largest number of mustangs were last seen. These horses probably had not been chased much. When they found them, they'd need a trap to hold them. But that would be worth doing only if there was some worthwhile horseflesh.

Using field glasses, they located several bands of mares and colts, each led by a stud horse. The older males were the ones he wanted, but they'd need to run them all in and separate them. It was likely to be a mess, and they'd almost certainly have to shoot some of the angry studs to control things before it was over. It wasn't pleasant, but that was simply part of mustang roundups. Young colts could be hurt and crippled in the panic, then need to be destroyed.

"We need to build some blinds to herd them to their final corrals. We can string up sheets or canvas to guide them that way. Since they haven't been run a lot, we'll need to hire a dozen more riders as day labor. I think we'll be able to get a good number in the pens."

Cur agreed. "There's a water hole they use just north of here. We'll need lots of high fences built. The back part's sheer bluff, so that'll help us out, but we'll need to get all the posts and rails cut first and make it really quick so our smell doesn't remain. No human pissing or crapping anywhere close to the corral by the builders."

They stepped off the corral's length and where the gates would be. Norm made notes, and Cur outlined the blinds they'd need set up to funnel the horses into the trap.

It was mid-afternoon when they started back to the ranch.

Norman looked to his foreman. "You have more experience at this. You feel this plan will get us the horses we need?"

"If it all goes well, we'll have lots more horses than we need, but it's the only way. We can sort them out after that."

Norm agreed. He knew, eventually, they'd have to clean up the mustangs. They ate the grass he'd someday need for his beef herd. But that could wait until they had more cattle. Right now, he needed saddle stock for the upcoming drive north.

That afternoon, Edith asked him if something was wrong—he was being awfully quiet.

He set down his newspaper, and stood. "You know we spied on the mustangs today. We're planning to build a large trap to catch some more useable horses. We'll need up to a hundred saddle horses for the drive north. But we'll be lucky to get two dozen useable mounts out of this. Those mustangs eat lots of grass, and someday we'll need to dispose of the rest. Wild horses have been here since the Spanish brought 'em, but ranching makes demands of the land, and we need all the grazing we can get. I just dread having to eliminate them someday."

"I understand, darling. It's a part of your big heart that stole mine." She gave him a kiss. "You care about everything, man and beast both. But you have the look of a tough cowboy. When you came by and asked to help me, I thought you were just another man to keep me in slavery. All I'd known, since I was raped and kidnapped were bad men. I thought they were all alike Using women, keeping them for their own purposes. I didn't know there were any other men left in the world who acted like you. My life was so bad among those outlaws—well, thank God you came and saved me. I was beaten and abused, and no one ever stepped in and stopped Elder or any of the others. I saw in you a savior, but I felt like I was grasping at a straw. Elder'd been in jail before, and he always broke out. But here was this big cowboy who knocked him on his butt and had him arrested.

"I knew when I joined you, that you were a sweet man. No one ever worried if they pleased me. You did, and I've had a great time, riding down here and fixing this mansion. No, Norman Thompson, you're a very tender man." She caressed his face. "I am so proud to be your wife and to have your son."

He tweaked her nose with his finger. "It still may be a girl."

They went outside and sat on a bench to watch the sunset, side by side.

He said softly, "I'll try not to think about that problem—or any other—until I have to."

The following week, men were hired to cut posts and corral rails, and the horse trap was laid out. Things moved fast from there.

Midweek another rider came in. Someone pointed him to Norm.

"Mister Thompson, I need a job. I know cattle, and I know the land between here and Kansas."

Norm looked him over. He appeared young and strong enough, but he kept his hat pulled low and wouldn't look him in the eye. Something wasn't quite right.

"I've pretty much got a full crew. I don't know if I can use another man."

The cowboy started to turn away. "That's usually what they say."

"Now, hold on just a minute, son. I didn't say yes or no. What did you mean by that last remark?"

"Nothing."

"Take that hat off a minute."

The man hesitated, then did as he'd been directed. At last, he looked him directly in the eye.

"Part Indian, are you?"

"Yes, sir. My ma was Quahadie."

"Comanche, huh? Well, that tells me you can ride, and you're tough enough to make the trip. You think you can take that chip off your shoulder till we get to Kansas?"

The young cowboy thought about it for a moment. "Yes, sir."

"You have any other skills I should know about?"

"Well, I'm a passable hand with a rope, but I'm really good with a horse. And I can track a lizard across a lava bed most days." He offered a big grin which didn't quite give the lie to his statements. "Could use some practice with my scalping knife, but that can wait."

"When did you eat last?"

"Yesterday, I think, but I'm okay."

"What's your name?"

"Best call me Blue. The other one's hard to pronounce."

"All right, Blue. Put your horse in the corral and come up to the house. Let's see if we can put enough weight on you so you don't blow out of the saddle."

"Yes, sir." He trotted off to the corral leading his horse. The big chestnut looked like a good piece of horseflesh.

He went in and asked Edith to have Modula fix a plate.

"You hungry again already?"

"No, it's for the new man I just hired. He'll be here in a minute."

"Do we need another man?"

"I think we might need this one."

A few minutes later, Blue knocked softly, and Norm called for him to come in. He introduced him to Edith.

"Hello, Blue." Edith shook the young man's hand. "Have a seat at the table. Modula is heating something up for you."

"Thank you, ma'am."

"Now, none of that. My name's Edith. We're not the least bit formal here."

"Yes, ma—Edith."

Modula brought a large bowl heaped with beans, a *tamale*, and fresh *tortillas*. Blue's eyes lit up like it was Christmas, and Norm exchanged a smile with Edith as she brought him a cup of coffee to go with it. She brought the sugar bowl and a spoon as well, having heard somewhere that Indians liked a lot of sugar in their coffee. Blue ignored it and drank his black.

"Take your time, Blue," said Norm. "Come see me when you're through, and I'll introduce you to the boys."

He took Edith by the arm and steered her into the parlor.

"He's Indian, isn't he?"

"Half. His ma was a Comanche."

"Do you think it's a good idea to hire him?"

"I think he's a young man trying hard to find his way and not quite fitting in either world. I think we can use him, and I'd like to give him a chance."

"Some of the men might not like it."

"Then they can draw their pay. No one decides who rides for the Rocking Chair but me and you."

Norm and Edith sat in the parlor drinking coffee until Blue came to find him. The young man thanked Edith for the fine meal and then walked with Norm out to the corral to meet Cur and some of the other boys.

"Cur, boys, this is Blue. I want him put in charge of the *remuda* for the drive north."

Cur shook hands with him, but the other two men just stared.

Phil Doone gave him a strange look. "Isn't that a big risk, Norm?"

"How so, Phil?"

"Kinda like putting the fox in charge of the chickens, ain't it?"

Out of the corner of his eye, Norm saw Blue tense up. He'd need to squash this quick before things got ugly.

He shook his head. "I don't think so, Phil. I decide who rides for Rocking Chair and what jobs they get assigned. I pick the best man for each job as I see it."

Phil wasn't through complaining "Well, it just don't set right with me."

"Well, son, Blue is our new hostler. You don't have to like it. You can always draw your time."

"No, sir, I reckon I'll stick."

"Fine. Not another word about it, and you can pass that to the other hands as well. Any man who doesn't want to ride with Blue can draw their pay."

Blue turned out to have a great way with horses, especially mustangs. Norm thought he was around sixteen, weighed under a hundred pounds soaking wet, and looked so slim he could slip through a picket fence. He rode an Indian bronc with only a blanket and a single rein tied on the red roan pony's jaw. He also had no interest in sleeping in the bunkhouse. Cur said the boy would be alright living in the brush, but they furnished him food.

Blue had all the various bands of mustangs mapped out just a few days later. He drew a diagram in the dirt with a stick and showed them all where each little group had staked their claim. He could count, and he told Cur, Rowdy, and Norm how many mares and colts were in each band. He also estimated the shunned males at forty. Those were the ones they wanted. After they were caught, they would need to be castrated, branded, and broke to ride.

"You should cut all the colts and brand them when we have them up."

Norm nodded. "Agreed. You're a great horse wrangler, son. I expect you'll come in handy on the trip north to the Strip."

A smile crossed his dark face when he shook Norm's hand. "Thank you. I want to go."

"Six weeks and they'll have the corral built," Cur said.

"We should have a horse roundup then?"

Blue stood. "Mister Thompson, let me ride after these horse bands before you do the roundup. I can get them used to me being behind them and they won't panic when all of us go to corral them. I'll just ride by and make them curious so by the end, they won't run from us."

"If you can do it, that would be fine."

Blue grinned big. "I'll have them trained."

"Do it."

"You want me to start now?"

"If you want to, sure. We'll need those mounts broken before we start rounding up the cattle."

Rowdy put his hands on his hips. "We about have all we need in the chuckwagon. Now we just need a real cook."

"I'll ask Edith. She and a few of the older Mexican girls can handle it."

"You sure?"

"She isn't that fancy. Get them a wall tent, cots, and a bathtub. I bet they'll do it. I'll go ask her."

Norm went back to the house and found her sewing. "We need a head cook, and I'll get you some teenage girls to help you cook for our first cattle roundup. Can you do it?"

"When?"

"Tomorrow."

She grinned. "You know I can. I better get packed. Modula, I'll need three teenage girls to help me cook for the roundup crew. You pick the ones that will work, and I'll get packed. Tell them we leave at sunup and will be gone ten days."

Norm nodded. "That should do it. There'll be a tent, cots, and a bathtub. They'll be paid, too. And no one will harm them. We'll follow it with a horse roundup just afterward."

When they broached the idea, Modula waved her hand to dismiss any doubt they might have had. "Oh, *señora,* I can get half a dozen."

"I'd be happy with three if they work hard."

By sundown, the chosen girls came to the house, and Modula introduced them. "Rita, Louise, and Carla. They are all excited."

Rita was small in stature with flashing eyes and a beguiling smile. Louise was taller, with a quiet demeanor, and when she laughed, she covered her mouth with her hand. Carla was a bigger girl, talkative, and prone to giggling. All were teens and seemed happy about the job opportunity. Louise spoke for all of them. "We are very happy to be your assistants, *Señora* Thompson."

"I appreciate you girls coming. But please, my name is Edith, *not Señora* Thompson. We will be working together. Bring your things. Blankets, it may be cool at night. Bring clothes to work in."

"*Gracias.* We will do as you ask."

After they left, Modula confided in Edith that the girls were wearing the only clothes they owned.

Edith reacted like the budding mother hen she was. "Oh, we'll change that tomorrow. There will be no more of that."

Modula smiled, and Norman did the same. No doubt in his mind, the girls would get a new wardrobe before he could snap his fingers.

Morning brought lots of scurrying around. Rowdy had a two-bench buckboard, and put their bedrolls and bundles in the chuckwagon. After discussions, he appointed Louise to drive it beside Edith.

Rowdy gave her some last-minute instruction. "Louise, these horses are very broke, you'll only have to flick them with the reins. They're safe and completely lazy."

Norm rode by and told Edith and her girls to follow the chuckwagon. Wiley, a sawed-off old man with maybe few two left in his head, was on the chuckwagon seat, getting the big black mule team ready to go. Cur told him to wait for the buckboard.

Around ten in the morning they arrived at the large meadow where they planned to set up camp. Cur had two younger hands collect firewood, bust it, and saw it in lengths they could use. Two other cowboys used hand-held sickles to mow the tall grass down to prevent a fire. Two more hauled rocks in to ring the fire and set up an iron cross bar to hang pots on. The girls greased the Dutch ovens, and when the fires were lit, boiled water and got some coffee going.

Wiley and the girls put up the canvas shade off the end of the tailgate to work under. Tables were set up and the benches unloaded. They heated up some precooked *frijoles* and cooked tender beef strips on a standing grill. Biscuits were already in the Dutch ovens to bake so that by noontime, they'd be ready.

Rita rang the triangle, and all the cowboys came in fast. Norm could see the men were all bragging about the good food they'd fixed so quickly. It was a funny situation, with men introducing themselves to the young female staff. Just real cowboys, some bashful, others talking and laughing, and others stood around silent. Edith oversaw it all with a watchful eye.

Norm put a hand on her shoulder. "You did well."

"No, these girls did it all. I just supervised. After everyone eats, we'll wash dishes and start on supper."

"I won't worry about it any longer."

She looked at the sky. "This isn't my first cookout. Remember, I fed plenty of outlaws all by myself."

CHAPTER No. 10

THEY DIVIDED THE ranch into pie-shaped sections, and the next morning, each group of hands rode to the far end of their assigned areas and brought all the cattle to the meadow. Edith sent fried apple pies with each man at midday, and the women set in to wash dishes and take a break before they started supper.

Norm caught sight of a cow with a small calf cutting back and headed his horse into the cedars. The pungent aroma and sticky needles swept his chaps and arms while he pushed his horse through the boughs. He cut her off on the far side. His mount scrambled on the talus rocks, but at last, he got in front of her. She soon moved west with a few more pairs and some maverick yearlings they'd gathered. There might be more cattle out here than they'd estimated. His torn shirtsleeve showed the scars of brush popping, but at least the mother cow and calf were in the fold.

Roby Hindsman laughed as Norm rejoined the group. "Hey, Phil, the boss man's going to have to ask his wife for a new shirt."

Buck-toothed Phil Doone laughed. "Was it this tough in Montana?"

"No. I rode under the pines and firs up there."

"They got cactus?"

"Not as much as grows down here. But they have beds of it, too."

"I took a herd of cows to Arizona once. Man, they've got more cactus out there than anything else. There's cactus tall as a two-story house, barrel cactus and jumping cactus that'll fly out and get you with ten thousand needles. After we got that herd delivered, I came right back to Texas. That place'll cook you. A hundred and ten degrees and no shade. It damn sure wasn't for me out there."

"Was there any grass?"

"Yeah, in some places. They say cattle do good when they learn what to eat. But boys, it ain't no paradise to me."

"So you just came home?"

"Yep. I—" A cagey cow started to break, and Phil broke off and sent his pony after her. The race was short, he headed her off, and the calf turned back.

"There's three pair heading south." Norm pointed. The cattle had seen them and took off the other way with their tails over their backs.

"I'll hold this bunch," Norm said, and the two took off.

He kept his group in the open meadow, and in a short while, the cowboys brought those eight head back in. By midafternoon they had a large group headed into the pasture.

Cur rode out to meet them. "How many you guys get?"

Norm nodded to the herd. "Forty-seven head."

"We have over a hundred head here, with one more bunch coming with Rowdy—maybe more than all these. Those guys that gathered the cattle for that close-out bank sale sure must have missed lots of them."

"To our good fortune and none of their own." Norm laughed, and everyone joined him.

Mixing cattle always called for a lot of pushing and shoving to establish who was the boss in the pecking order. These were no different than any other collection, and even the bulls got bossy. Extra riders kept them in the center, though, and they settled down around a small live water creek to drink and bawl some more.Phil and Roby rode out to help Rowdy with the last bunch. The rest of the riders kept the herd held in the large meadow.

When they returned, Edith frowned at his shirt. "You got caught?"

"You tear up a few things popping brush."

"I can repair it. Rita, get my sewing kit." The girl trotted off. Edith turned back to him. "These girls are such big helpers. I enjoy them, and I know the cowboys like them—they're flirting all the time. All I need to do is make the plans for the meals, and they can do it all. They're very dedicated and careful."

By sundown, Rowdy and his bunch brought in a hundred more head. The Rocking Chair herd was going to be impressive in numbers, Norm and his foremen agreed.

That night, lying on a pallet beside Edith, she asked him if he was pleased with the start of the roundup operation.

"I have to be. We could have four to five hundred head of stock. This is a large ranch and lots more to cover."

"Good. And don't worry about me, I'm having fun, too. I'll fix your shirt better tomorrow. You have another to wear." She smiled at him. "Tomorrow, the women are all getting baths, so don't come back too soon. I don't want you catching a glimpse and thinking you might want someone younger and prettier."

"No chance of that, my dear."

T HEY BROUGHT IN fewer cattle the next day but gathered a hundred and fifty head. That meant three-fifty althogether. The plan was now to brand, use his earmark, and cut the bulls. Fires were built and stoked to heat irons. Three heelers roped the calves by the hind legs and drug them to the nearest fire, where the hands flanked them and kept them still. They used a bar to cross out the two different brands rustlers had put on six of his calves, and his men remarked them.

Norm wrote down both brands, the GY Brand and a Star—neither one he knew. He planned to look the owners up, though. This was outright rustling, and the brand owners had to answer to those charges. Unpleasant, but part of owning a ranch.

The next day they wound up the branding for the first section and moved on north. Late afternoon, they arrived at the new campsite, and everyone helped Edith's crew get set up. They had a meal of stew ready to reheat for supper, and afterwards it was another quiet night under the stars.

The roundup began again at dawn. This drive brought in three hundred more head, and during branding, they found twelve of the calves illegally branded by the late Meaders brothers.

They moved on west. This was the real cattle country, and they brought in four hundred eighty head. Before they returned to the homestead, they'd put twelve hundred head in the herd book. The cowboys were in high spirits on the dim road going back home, and they teased the girls riding in the buckboard and told jokes and stories as they rode. Modula and Mattie ran out to greet them as they rode up.

Norm told all the cowboys that he'd advance them all ten bucks for the successful cattle roundup and give them three days to go raise hell in town. The single ones threw their hats in the air. They didn't need to be told twice—in ten minutes they were ready to head for town and blow their pay on whiskey and flesh.

Norm signaled Cur that he needed a word.

"Whatcha need, boss?"

"I hate to be a wet blanket, but I need you, Rowdy, along with two more men, to stick around the ranch till the boys get back. I'll see that you get your turn after."

"Aw, hell, Norm. I'm getting a bit long in the tooth to be chasing girls and playing poker all night. I'll grab the others before they bolt. I think we might have a couple who aren't all that social, anyway."

"Thanks, Cur."

Edith paid her helpers ten dollars apiece, as well. She was nearly hugged to death. Most of the women had never seen that kind of money before. They told her to call on them any time she needed assistance. In turn, she thanked them and promised she would.

Things would be slow for a while with the boys in town and the rest healing from roundup. Rowdy had the youngest cowboy go find Blue and tell him that they'd start the horse roundup when the rest of the hands came back.

The large ranch herd had been a windfall and a start on making it a working ranch. There was more work coming, though, and Norm asked his wife if she could get her girls together again for the horse roundup cook duty.

"I don't think we'll have any problem convincing them."

CHAPTER No. 11

THE NEXT MORNING after breakfast, Norm asked Edith to make a list of the supplies she needed from town.

"Oh, Norm. Can I go with you? It's been ages since I went to town."

Looking at her eager expression, he couldn't bring himself to say no. "You can, but I warn you. I may have to leave you there for a day or two while I take care of my business."

"I don't mind going wherever you go. You know I can ride."

"We'll see, but you've been warned."

"You sound so ominous. What is it?"

"I don't know for sure yet, but I promise you a pleasant trip. You deserve it. Now, go pack what you might need for two or three days."

Norm walked out to the corral and found Cur watching one of the boys take the kinks out of a saddlehorse.

"Morning, Cur. I need one of the boys to hitch a team to the buckboard."

"Going into town?"

"Yep. Edith needs a few things, and she wants to get out of the house for a bit."

"You got it, boss."

"And, Cur—whoever you choose'll be driving the rig to town and back."

"Sure. Want to tell me what's shaking?"

"Edith is going shopping, and your man's going to watch over her. You and I are going to see the marshal and try to get a line on those would-be rustlers who branded our cattle."

"I wondered when you'd get around to that. Give me ten minutes, and I'll have our horses saddled and the buckboard hitched." Cur headed for the barn, yelling as he went, "Carleton, quit holding up that fence and get over here. Boss has got a job for you."

As Cur went to fill Wylie Carleton in on their plans, Norm went back to the house. He found Edith in the parlor explaining to Modula where they were going and when they'd return.

"*Señora,* do not worry. We will take care of everything. You go. Have a good time."

"I know you will, Modula. I have complete faith in you. Mostly, I worry that you will work too hard. Take time to enjoy some coffee now and then."

"*Si, Señora.* We will be fine, and I have the girls if I need them."

Norm picked up Edith's carpetbag off the settee.

"Lord, what do you have in here, gold bricks?" He set it back down and opened it as she rushed to stop him. He held her back with one arm and lifted a .36 Navy Colt out of the bag. Rummaging around in the bag, he found a powder horn and a large bag of conical bullets. "You planning on going hunting or something?"

"Norm, I know what you're planning. You're going after those rustlers, and I can help."

"You can help by staying where I don't have to worry about you. You can do that here or in town, but if I get a lead on those rustlers, I don't want to worry that you might be in the line of fire. Cur's going along to back my play, and Wylie Carleton's driving the wagon and staying in town with you. Maybe he can keep you from shooting someone."

Modula tried to hide her giggle behind her hand without much success.

"Alright, damn you. If Cur's going with you, I suppose you won't need my services as a gunfighter… this time. I'll promise to be good if you'll promise not to get yourself killed."

"All right. Now that's settled, are you ready to go?"

"You lead, and I'll follow," she said with a twinkle in her eye.

Norm scooped her up and twirled around before planting a deep kiss on her lips. "I love you, Edith Thompson."

"And I love you, Norman Thompson. Shall we go?"

Norm dropped the armaments back in the carpetbag with a wink, and they walked out to the wagon Wylie had brought around to the porch steps. Norm dropped the valise in the back and helped Edith up on the wagon.

Cur flipped his reins to him, and he mounted up and led the way out the ranch gate turning toward town.

Cur rode beside him and leaned in close. "Any idea how we're going to find these jaspers?"

"I figure we'll ask the marshal if he recognizes the brands. If not, we may have to go to the Cattlemen's Association in San Antonio to see who registered them."

"As good a place as any to start."

With her usual knack for putting folks at ease, Edith struck up a conversation with Wylie, which soon had them both laughing and exchanging funny stories. That suited Norm fine. He couldn't get enough of her laughter.

When they got to town, Norm got two rooms at the hotel across the hall from each other. The clerk said he'd see to it that Edith's bag was placed in their room, and she headed out to do her shopping.

Norm buttonholed Wylie after she walked out the door. "Wylie, why don't you take the buckboard and horses over to the stable and put 'em up, then head over to the saloon. They'll be having a free lunch soon. Stick to beer, because you may be needed to watch over Edith."

"Yes, sir. I appreciate it."

Norm and Cur tied their horses to the back of the wagon and pulled their saddle guns. "We'll meet you there in a little while. C'mon, Cur. Let's go see what the marshal can tell us."

They walked down the boardwalk and knocked at the door.

"Come on in," a voice said from inside.

Norm opened the door and walked in, Cur following on his heels. "Marshal?"

"That's me. Marshal Tom Kitridge, and you're Norm Thompson. I don't know that jasper behind you."

"This is Cur Taylor, my foreman."

"Glad to meetcha." The marshal shook their hands. "What can I do for you, Mister Thompson?"

"I was wondering if you recognized a couple of brands I came across."

"Maybe. What are they?"

"A GY and a Star."

"Well, the GY I can help you with. It belongs to your neighbor to the south, George Yoder. Why do you ask?"

"I found a couple of my cows nursing calves with those brands on 'em."

"That don't sound like something George would do. He's small potatoes next to your place, but all his dealings have been honest and above board so far as I know. Do you want me to speak to him?"

"No. I'll take your word that it's an honest mistake, and we'll discuss it man to man. I have an idea we can come to an agreement. What about that Star brand?"

"It's not one I recognize from around here. Be a good one for blotting other brands with, though."

"That's sort of what I figured. Anyone around here you might suspect of such things?"

"No one comes to mind, but I'll sure keep my eyes and ears open. If some-one's getting free and easy with their branding, I'll hear about it."

"You just did, but I'd appreciate you keeping an eye out."

They shook hands again and left the office. On the boards outside, Cur asked, "What now?"

Walking off a little way from the marshal's office, Norm tilted his head toward the far end of town. "What's say we go see if the smithy maybe knows something?"

They headed down to the end of the street across from the stable and found the blacksmith shoeing a big Percheron gelding. He dunked the hot shoe in a trough and held it up to the horse's hoof to check the fit.

The big man put the shoe and his tongs down and turned to face them. "You boys need a horse shod?"

"Not today. I'm interested in a branding iron. You make those?"

"I can, and I have, but I don't get much call for them. Most folks make their own. What brand you need?"

"I'm interested in one that looks like this." Norm squatted and drew a star in the dirt.

The blacksmith gave a start, which he tried to hide, but Norm and Cur both noticed. Before he could fully recover, Norm pressed him. "You make one like this for someone around here?"

"No. Can't say as I have."

"Mister, my name's Norm Thompson. I own the Rocking Chair. Believe me when I say you'd much rather have my business than the man you made that iron for."

"I told you, I didn't make no such iron, and I don't appreciate you calling me a liar."

"Alright, so you didn't make it. My mistake. Where have you seen it?"

"Don't rightly recall."

"Cur, why don't you trot back to the marshal and ask him to join us?"

"Now, hang on. Gimme a minute, and I may figure out where I've seen it."

Norm held up his hand to keep Cur from going.

"There's an old man, Emmet something or other. I don't recall if I heard his last name. He's got him a piddly little two-bit spread about twenty miles west of here up in the hills. Maybe has fifteen or twenty scrawny cows. His son, Lonnie, was in town about a month ago. He was spending more than he should have and bragging as to how, in two or three years, his old man's spread would be the biggest around. When he went to pay for a round of drinks, a slip of paper fell out of his pocket. That brand was on it."

"Is it Emmet's brand?"

"No. He's a Box3. That's why I remembered it. Seemed strange that Lonnie would have his own brand."

"Thank you, Mister...?"

"Gordon. Big Jim Gordon."

"Thank you, Mister Gordon. I'm going to be drilling some wells out on the Rocking Chair. I'll need some good sharp drill bits. Can you handle that?"

"Sure. How many, and when do you need them?"

"Better have half a dozen. Three weeks give you enough time?"

"I'll have 'em. They'll be three bucks apiece."

"Fifteen for all six, and you got a deal."

"Done."

They shook hands to seal the deal, and Norm led the way over to the livery stable. There, he arranged for a bag of grain for both his horse and Cur's before leading the way to the saloon to meet Wylie. They found him alone at a table with a mug of beer he was nursing and a plate of free lunch. It looked good.

"Hey, Wylie."

"Howdy, boss. You fellas want a beer?"

"I'll pass for now. Still a bit early, and I need to see that Edith has some lunch. Yours looks good, though. I'll buy you both one, and Cur can eat with you." He caught the barkeeper's eye, pointed at Wylie's beer, and held up two fingers. The bartender nodded and reached for a couple mugs.

"You heard anything?"

Wylie shook his head. "No, there've been some fellas in and out, but nobody said anything that made my ears perk up."

"We've got two names we're sure are connected to those calves. George Yoder's a cowman south of here. I'm gonna ride out and speak to him tomorrow. The other one, we only have a first name, Lonnie. Seems he's behind the Star brand or somehow associated with it. Keep your ears open and see if you hear anything about him or his pa. Father's name is Emmet. Meanwhile, you two can have the rest of the day off. Stay out of trouble and meet us for breakfast at the café down the street."

"Sure thing, boss."

About then, the bartender brought the beers. Norm indicated they were for the hands and paid for the drinks. He told the boys to have a good night and followed the barman back to the bar.

"Was there something else, sir?"

"Some information if you have it." Norm placed a five-dollar gold piece on the bar but kept his finger on it.

The bartender eyed the coin, then made up his mind. "What do you want to know?"

"Anything you can tell me about an older man named Emmet and his son, Lonnie? I believe the kid was in here not too long ago."

"That trash? Don't know much about them. The old man is quiet enough. Mostly keeps to himself and don't come to town but four or five times a year. Tight with his money, but pays his bills. Came down here from the Tennessee hill country, I heard. He don't brag, but he totes an old rifle with him, and I suspect he can use it. If you're asking my opinion, he don't look for trouble, but he'd be tough as nails if you pushed him."

Norm nodded. "And the kid?"

"Lonnie's a worthless loudmouth. Comes in a lot more often than his old man. Likes to wear a tied-down gun and talk tough, but he always veers off before someone challenges him to gunplay. There's been a couple cowboys and gamblers roughed up and robbed, and Lonnie was suspected, but no one could prove it." The man looked pointedly at the coin.

"Just one more question. What can you tell me about George Yoder?"

"Don't even mention George along with them other two. He's the salt of the earth. Grew up around here and worked hard to make it. He's got him a small spread just south of here. Works hard, minds his own business, goes to church every Sunday. His wife usually wins something at the County Fair for her cooking and canning. He's got three or four kids, all too young to give him a hand with his cattle, but they stay out of trouble and are respectful to adults."

"Thanks. That's about what I figured." Norm pushed the coin across the counter and released it. The barkeep swept it up and nodded.

Norm left the saloon and walked the boards looking in various store windows. He found Edith in the dress shop and went in.

"Well, do I need to fetch the wagon for your purchases?"

"No. I think we can manage to carry them if you're not worn out already."

Edith paid for her packages, and Norm picked up the paper-wrapped bundle bound with string from the counter before escorting her out the door.

"Too worn out, huh?" He gave her a saucy grin. "Maybe we should go back to the hotel and test that theory."

"We could do that, but I promised to take care of my man, and I need to see that he's fed first. Perhaps we could meet at the hotel later?"

Norm laughed. "That sounds like a fine idea. There's a café right down the street here if that suits you."

"That sounds fine, sir." She smiled, and he couldn't hold back any longer. He picked her up and kissed her hard right there.

When he put her down, Edith fanned her face. "Well, sir. Now that you've ruined my reputation, you'll have to feed and care for me."

Norm laughed. "I think I can do that."

After a light lunch, they returned to the hotel, where Edith agreed he really wasn't worn out after all. They napped and lazed about until suppertime.

Norm had made reservations for them in the hotel dining room. To be honest, the fare wasn't much better than the café, but the tables had tablecloths on them, and the flatware was a little fancier. The coffee cups had saucers, and the wineglasses had stems.

It turned out that the package from the dress shop was a new dress. It was a lovely pale blue with a matching bow in the back and a scalloped ecru overskirt edged in lace.

When she tried it on, it took Norm's breath away. "Edith, I'm going to look positively seedy next to you in that dress."

"Oh, you. I think you look a fine figure of a man. Well, maybe a bit dusty and trail worn, but a fine figure, nonetheless."

Before Norm could reply to her teasing, there was a knock at the door. Norm answered it to find the desk clerk holding a new suit on a wooden hanger. It was a soft grey pinstripe.

Edith stepped up beside him, tipped the clerk, and took the suit. "Thank you very much."

"I guess that new dress wasn't all the shopping you did today, huh?"

"Well, I couldn't have my man looking seedy next to my new dress, could I? Besides, part of being a successful cattleman is the image. You have to dress the part."

"You are always full of charming surprises, my dear."

Norm tried the suit on and was pleased to see that it fit nearly perfectly.

She looked him up and down. "It needs a couple of minor alterations, but it will do for tonight. I can adjust it when we're back home."

"Shall we go down to dinner, madame?" Norm offered her his arm.

"Yes, but first you must kiss me."

He was only too happy to comply.

The waiter seated them at a table with a nice view of the street but not so close as to make them feel like they were on display. They ordered steaks with pintos and greens.

"So, tell me about your day."

"Well, I've got leads on both of the brands we found on our calves."

"Really? So fast?"

"Yes. The GY is a small rancher, George Yoder. Lives south of us. He's got a good reputation. Don't know why his brand would be on our calves, but I'll go talk to him tomorrow."

"What about the Star brand?"

"That one's a little more complicated. Seems there's an old Tennessee mountain man and his family living west of us a way. Don't think he's involved, but somehow his son is. The boy's got a reputation for trouble. From what I know of those hill folks, they're clannish. Might be a tough job, cutting the kid out of the herd."

A big, slightly heavyset man stepped up to their table. He removed his hat and nodded to Edith.

"Ma'am. Excuse me for the interruption." He turning to Norm. "I hear you're looking for me. My name's George Yoder."

Norm stood up and offered his hand.

"Pleased to meet you, Mister Yoder. Won't you join us? I want to talk cattle with you."

"I don't want to interrupt your meal. Might be better if we talked after." He looked pointedly at Edith.

"Sorry, Mister Yoder. May I introduce my wife, Edith. Edith, this is George Yoder."

"Pleased to meet you Mister Yoder."

"I know it isn't customary, Yoder, but my wife is as much a part of the Rocking Chair operations as I am. We can speak freely in front of her."

"In that case, I'll accept your invitation."

Norm signaled for the waiter. "Please, take Mr. Yoder's order and put it on my bill. He'll be joining us."

"Yes, sir."

"I'll have what they're having and a cup of coffee, young man."

"Make that coffee for all of us," said Edith.

"Yes, ma'am. Right away."

"So, Yoder, how did your round-up go this year?" Norm took his napkin off the table and placed it in his lap.

"So, so. I only have a couple of full-time hands and can't afford to pay much, so I ended up with a small crew of less than top hands. We got her done, though."

"You have a market for your steers?"

"Well, I had a buyer at Fort Inge until they shut it down. Reckon I'll drive them to Fort Clark and see if I can sell them there."

"How many head do you have for sale?"

"It's a small herd. Probably four hundred, maybe four-fifty."

"The Army pays what, fifteen or sixteen dollars a head?"

"I'm looking for eighteen."

"Tell you what, I've got two herds going north in a few weeks. I've already bought what I need, but I can handle four or five hundred more. You drive them over to my place. We'll get an exact count while we trail brand them, and I'll pay you eighteen on the spot. Or you can drive them over, and I'll give you a receipt for them. We'll take them north with us, and I'll sell them for you in Kansas at fifty or more per head."

"What's the catch?"

"The catch is, that we're only taking two-year-olds and holding them in the Strip, so they'll be nice and fat for market in the spring."

"Hell—sorry, ma'am. I don't have anything but two-year-olds. I've sold all my older stock just to keep going. This could make all the difference for my ranch. You've got yourself a deal. And please, call me George."

"Okay, George." Norm shook the offered hand. "That wasn't what I wanted to talk to you about though."

"Oh? What was?"

"Well, it's a sensitive matter, but bear with me and let me tell you what I think happened."

"All right."

"During our roundup last week, we found a few of our cows nursing calves with your brand on them." Norm held up his hand to keep George from busting in. "What I think happened, is you hired some hands with not too much experience, and they set out to brand what they could catch. I think that when they started to drive these calves to your ranch, the cows sort of tagged along. I think either these boys thought better of it, or one of your regular hands found out and had them driven back our way. In any case, I have no reason to believe that you had anything to do with it or even knew about it, and I've put a bar through those GY brands and rebranded them, so there's no harm done."

"Mister Thompson, I'm ashamed to think that any man I hired would have done such a thing, but I don't have a better explanation."

"As I said, no harm done. Why don't we get together next year and coordinate one big roundup for the whole range? It'll save time, payroll, and prevent any misunderstandings. We'll do all the branding together with a rep from your place, my place, and any smaller outfits who want to participate watching over the whole shebang."

"I'd like that just fine, Norm." They shook hands again as their steaks arrived. They smelled delicious as they sizzled on their plates.

After a pleasant dinner, Norm declined the offer of a drink and took Edith back to their room.

"I thought that went really well, Norm."

"I expected it to. He's an honest man just trying to make a living, same as anyone else."

"Yes, and the joint roundup will prevent any possible future misunderstandings. I like it."

They met the hands for breakfast at the café the next morning, then went to get their horses and wagon for the trip back to the ranch.

As Norm helped Edith up onto the wagon seat, she poked his shoulder "Don't forget we need to get those supplies for Cookie."

"Good point. Wylie, take Missus Thompson down to the store. We'll join you as soon as we get saddled."

CHAPTER No. 12

A FEW DAYS LATER, Norm kissed Edith goodbye, and with his bedroll under his arm and saddlebags over his shoulder, went to get his horse. Cur led their saddled mounts out of the corral. Putting the saddlebags on his animal, Norm tied the bedroll behind his saddle.

As he was mounting, Gunny Johnson galloped into the ranch yard, sliding to a stop on a lathered horse. "We got troubles, boss."

"What kind of trouble?"

"Rowdy sent me out to check the herd and tell the boys to move them a bit north for fresh graze. Everything seemed okay, but I cut to the west to chase a couple of strays back to the herd and found tracks."

"What kind of tracks?"

"Looked like about a dozen head or so headed due west."

"Well, did you go round them up?"

"No, sir. They wasn't straying. They was being driven."

"Blue." Norm hollered for his wrangler. "Hey, Blue! Get Gunny a fresh horse, will ya? Pronto!"

Blue grabbed a bridle off the corral fence, walked right up to a big chestnut, and slipped it on him. Dropping the reins, he got a saddle and blanket off the fence and put them on as well. The horse stood still as a statue except for an occasional head bob.

Gunny gaped. "If I hadn't seen it, I'd have never believed it."

"Boy does have a way with horses." Cur chuckled and shook his head.

Blue led the horse over and traded reins with Gunny. "I'll walk him until he's cool, Mister Gunny. You want your rifle and bedroll off him?"

Norm nodded assent, and Gunny transferred the items to the Chestnut and climbed into the saddle.

"Alright, Gunny. Show us these tracks." Norm turned his horse, and they rode out. They'd only ridden a mile or so when they heard a rider coming behind them. They waited to see who it was.

Turned out to be Blue.

"What are you doing here? I thought you were cooling Gunny's horse."

"I was, but Mister Rowdy said you might need a tracker. Said he'd get someone else to walk the horse."

Norm couldn't argue with that. "Well, Rowdy has a good idea ever now and then. Come on."

Gunny led them to a dry wash about three miles out from the ranch. As they entered the little swale, Blue kicked his horse to a trot and went out in front a few yards looking at the trail in the bottom of the wash. In seconds, he held up his hand, signaling a stop. He got off his horse and walked along for about twenty feet before re-mounting and returning to the party.

"Looks like a dozen or so cows. Two riders. Sometime late yesterday."

"Alright, Blue. You lead the way." Norm looked around at his men. "Everyone keep an eye peeled. If they're stealing our cows, they'll likely run or fight when we catch them."

They followed the dry creekbed west a couple more miles until it started to narrow. The trail turned south up over the edge of the wash, then west again. It entered an area of hardpan with little to no vegetation, and Blue signaled another halt while he rode in a circle to pick up the trail again. He was about a half mile northwest of them when he signaled that he'd found it.

"Thought you'd try tracking them across the rock," said Norm when they caught up to him.

"Too slow. Faster to circle and find where they come out. They're headed for those hills over there."

"How far ahead are they?"

"Eight, maybe ten hours."

"Alright. Let's push on." Norm wiped the sweat from his hatband and forehead with a bandana.

They rode on across the wide plains toward the hills ahead with nothing in sight except an occasional antelope or jackrabbit. Norm dug some jerky out of his saddlebag and shared it among the men.

The sun beat down on the party like a relentless furnace. Horses started to slow, showing signs of fatigue. At Norm's urging, they switched from riding to alternately riding and walking to give the horses a break. Blue dropped back to ride beside Norm.

Norm glanced over at him. "We need to find water for these horses and give them a break soon."

"There is water in the hills."

"You know where?"

The boy nodded gravely. "I know."

"Can we make it by sundown?"

"I think so."

It became a race against the clock to reach the shelter of the hills and find water before nightfall made movement too dangerous. Men and horses plodded on, heads down, feet and hooves dragging across the harsh landscape.

The sun was balanced on the horizon when they reached the hills.

"How far to the water?"

"Not far. We have another problem, though."

"What?"

"Come. You see."

Blue led his horse off the trail a bit to the north with Norm following. He pointed to a slightly sandy spot next to a mesquite clump.

"*Numinu*. The people."

"Comanches?"

Norm examined the tracks of an unshod pony. "Yes."

"Have they seen us?"

Blue shook his head. "No, but they have seen the cattle."

"How many of them?"

"Ten, maybe twelve. They follow the cows."

"And they're between us and the water?"

"No. Cow thieves don't know about the water. They are driving somewhere else."

"Blue, I know it's been difficult for you with one foot in this world and the other in theirs. I've got to know, now, though. It's time for you to decide. If it comes to a fight, where will you be?"

Blue hesitated, obviously considering the question. After nearly a minute, he looked up, staring Norm in the eye. "I ride for the brand."

"I believe you." Norm offered his hand, and they shook. "Let's get to that water, and we'll make plans when we get there."

Norm led the way back to the men.

"All right, boys. I'm gonna lay it on the line. Blue just showed me where there are at least ten Comanche following our cows. We're in their country, and they have the advantage of numbers. I'd like to get those cows back, but they're not worth any one of you. If we're attacked, we'll fight, and before anyone asks, Blue gave me his word he'll fight with us. That's good enough for me and the last word on the subject."

He looked from man to man and both nodded their agreement.

"That's the bad news. The good news is that the rustlers don't know about the waterhole, so they're leading the Comanche away from us. I'm for pressing on to water, and we'll decide then what to do next."

"Sounds good to me," said Gunny.

"You're the boss." Cur stepped into his saddle.

Blue led them around a small hill and into a rocky canyon. Their progress was occasionally impeded by thick mesquite or large boulders, but they found ways around. The canyon walls grew steeper and pressed in on them. After a mile or so, Blue held up a hand, and they stumbled to a halt behind him.

"Walk from here, but go slow and make no noise."

Norm looked around in the darkness. "Something wrong?"

"Nothing yet, but water is close by. The tracks we saw may not be the only *Numinu* in these hills. The ground is bad from here. Much rocks. I will make sure there are no others there."

Blue turned and disappeared into the shadows.

"I sure hope you're right about him," Cur said in a low voice.

Gunny shook his head. "Don't you worry about that. When a Comanche gives his word, he'll die before he breaks it. That's good enough for me."

"All right, Blue said to keep it quiet. Let's do that." Norm pulled his rifle from his saddle scabbard. "It might be a good idea to keep our rifles in hand, though. Gunny, you lead Blue's horse with yours."

The three men proceeded up the narrowing canyon in the gathering twilight, working their way around boulders and over rocks. They cringed each time an iron-shod hoof struck a stone. Pausing often to listen, knowing that their ears and those of their horses were their best warning of any impending danger, they moved slowly and cautiously.

Lord, he hoped this wasn't a box canyon. If it was, they might play hob getting back out. They had gone about a half mile since parting with Blue when Norm signaled another halt. Something wasn't right, but he couldn't quite put his finger on it.

Cur eased up beside him. "What is it, boss?"

"Don't know. Maybe just an uneasy feeling."

Cur peered into the shadows ahead, and Gunny raised his head slightly, almost like he was sniffing the breeze.

"Maybe you make a good Comanche." Blue stepped from the shadows not six feet away. The men all let out a sigh of relief.

Norm hadn't realized he'd been holding his breath. "What did you find?"

"The water is good, and it safe to go in. You should leave one man here to watch our backtrail, and we should leave this place as soon as we can. *Numinu* will fight hard for water."

"I'll stay and keep watch," said Cur.

"Okay. We'll water the horses, including yours, then come back for you."

Less than a hundred yards up the canyon, Blue led them to a spring with a small pool at its base. The water was clear and cold. They quickly refilled all four canteens, had a drink, then let the horses water, making sure they didn't drink too much and founder.

"I'd really like to wait an hour and let them drink again," Norm said, "but you're right. It's too dangerous to hang around a waterhole in this country. Is there another way out of this place?"

Blue smiled. "It would be a good trap if there wasn't. If we stay close to the rock face, there is a path over the ridge to the next valley. I think we will pick up the trail of the others there. Maybe follow them, maybe go home."

Norm frowned. "Maybe run right into some Comanche coming for water."

"Maybe so, but the danger is less than going back the way we came."

"Agreed. Will you go get Cur?"

Blue nodded and trotted off. In less than twenty minutes, they were leading their horses over the rocky ridge and into the next canyon. Suddenly, Blue turned to the right and led them along a narrow ledge well above the canyon floor. They followed it around a bend in the canyon, where the ledge widened considerably.

Blue halted. "We rest here until daylight."

"Why here?"

"We are off the trail, hidden, where we can both see and hear anyone who comes."

The kid had a good head for this kind of thing, that was clear. "Good. We'll take turns on sentry watching the ledge beyond the bend and listening for movement in the canyon."

Morning arrived without incident, and the four men on the ledge tightened their girths and resumed their weary plodding hike into the next canyon. Norm shared the last of his jerky with the men. When they reached the canyon floor, they found tracks right away indicating that the cattle, rustlers, and Comanche had all passed this way headed up-canyon. They turned their horses following the tracks. All of them rode with their rifles across their saddlebows. They rode in silence, observing every crevice along the canyon walls and each bit of mesquite and brush growing in the bottom.

Mid-morning, they rounded another bend in the canyon and found them. Two pathetic white bodies lay in the sun, scalped and mutilated. Looking at them, Norm felt like he might be sick. He signaled a halt while Blue dismounted and led his horse forward to read the signs. There were no horses or cattle present.

Blue motioned them forward. Both men had suffered multiple wounds from bullets and arrows. Both wore empty holsters. Taking a deep breath, Norm went through their pockets to see if he could find any identification. There was nothing on the older man. The younger one had a receipt in his pocket for ten steers purchased from Mr. Lonnie Eakin and signed by the Post Sutler at Fort McKavett. Apparently, young Lonnie had received a hundred and eighty dollars for them.

"So, now we know where the bastards were taking our steers. There's probably a place between here and there where they waited for the fresh brands to heal, but we'll never find it. What do you think happened to the steers, Blue?"

"Comanche take them. Ten days they will be in Llano Estacado, maybe so."

"All right. No point in chasing them. We're outmanned and outgunned. Let them have the beef this time. Let's go home."

Cur nudged one of the bodies with his foot. "We gonna bury these boys?"

Norm felt his lip curl. "Would they have buried us? No point in announcing that we've been here. Let 'em rot."

They mounted and headed back down the canyon, still watchful for any threats. Exiting the ravine in the early afternoon, they turned southeast toward home. They'd ridden about an hour when they spotted a dust cloud northeast of them coming their way. Norm led them into a large mesquite thicket where they dismounted and waited to see who it was. In a few minutes, they could see that it was a sizeable party riding two-abreast.

Blue's jaw got tight when he saw them. "Soldiers."

"It's all right, Blue. You stay here out of sight. I don't want any trouble with the Army. We'll ride out and meet them."

Blue nodded, and the other three men exited the thicket and walked their horses toward the column. When they arrived, the young captain ordered a halt and rode forward to meet them.

"Captain Frank Dodge, Company G, 9th U.S. Cavalry at your service, gentlemen. What brings you out in this forsaken land?"

"We've been chasing rustlers, Captain."

"I presume you lost them in the hills?"

"You might say that. We found their bodies."

"Bodies?"

"Yes. Two men. Killed, scalped, and butchered. About three miles up that canyon back there."

"Might be the Comanche raiders we're pursuing. When did this happen?"

"Near as I can tell, yesterday, probably late in the day."

"Any idea who they were?"

"No idea on the older one. The younger was a kid named Lonnie Eakin. His pa owns the Box3 in the hills about twenty miles west of the Guadalupe. I'll notify him. You might put in your report that he was rebranding the stolen steers and selling them to the sutler at McKavett."

"I assume you have proof of this."

"I found this on the body." Norm pulled the receipt out of his pocket.

"I will indeed put this in my report and bring it to the Colonel's attention. May I keep this receipt?"

"I have no need of it. You may want to bury them two when you find them. We figured it was best to get out of there and leave as little sign of our passing as possible since we were heavily outnumbered."

"A very wise decision under the circumstances. Do you have some military experience?"

Norm scuffed a boot in the grass. "I held a battlefield commission under Forrest back in the war."

"Interesting fellow, Forrest. We studied him at the Point."

"You could do worse."

"Yes. Well, if that's all, I'll leave you gentlemen and see what I can do about pursuing the hostiles."

"You might catch them. They'll be slowed by a dozen steers, and they're headed for the Llano."

"Thank you, sir. Good day."

The captain rode back to his troopers, gave a command, and the three cowboys watched in wonder as a full company of buffalo soldiers rode west toward the canyon they'd just left.

Norm and his two cowboys walked their horses southeast until Blue caught up to them, then spurred into an easy lope toward home. They crossed the hills west of the Rocking Chair and found the Box3. The blacksmith had been right. It wasn't much more than ten cows and a dream. They rode up to the dooryard without seeing anyone.

"Hello, the house." Norm shouted it loud enough that anyone inside could hear—anybody with ears, at least.

The door opened, and a bushy-headed old man came out carrying an ancient Kentucky rifle.

"I see ya. No need to raise a ruckus. What do ya want?"

"Are you Mister Eakins?"

"I reckon I am."

"My name is Norm Thompson. I'm afraid I've got some bad news."

"Well, spit it out. I ain't got the whole day fer jawing."

"Your son, Lonnie, is dead."

"Did you kill him?"

"No, sir. I didn't."

"Then how'd you know he's dead?"

"Someone stole some of my cattle off the Rocking Chair. We rode after them. Tracked them into the badlands northwest of here. That's where we found your son. Comanches got him."

"Why didn't you bring him back here?"

"Mister Eakins, you really wouldn't want to remember him the way we found him. Besides, there were four of us and more than a dozen Comanches up that canyon and no spare horse to pack him back on. We ran into an army patrol, and they promised to give him a proper burial."

"Thankee fer bringing word. Now, I got work to do."

Norm nodded. There was nothing more to say.

He turned his mount, and they rode home to the Rocking Chair.

Edith must have seen them coming, because she flew out the door and into his arms almost before he dismounted.

"Oh, Norm. I was so worried. You look exhausted." She looked at the others. "All of you look exhausted. Wash up and come in the house, all of you. We have food on the table and fresh coffee."

"Just as soon as we take care of our horses."

"Rowdy!" Edith called for him, and he came running.

"Get someone to care for these horses. I'm taking the men up to the house."

"Yes, ma'am."

"Well, since you seem to have everything under control, ma'am," said Norm wryly, "I guess we're your prisoners."

The four men shuffled up onto the porch and washed up while Edith went in and started giving directions to Modula.

CHAPTER No. 13

THE RANCH HANDS came home hung over and exhausted, so the ride out to the new horse camp was a lot less fun than the ride out to the cattle camp the week before. Every step of their horses set them to moaning. Cur stayed home on the ranch to watch over things in their absence, and to help Margarita through her coming childbirth. Before they rode out, Norm made sure his right-hand man had a well-armed defense force to help him out.

They set up camp on a live stream. Blue pointed out which group to herd in first. A big paint stallion ran the bunch, and a leggy Kentucky mare led them. She had tremendous speed, and the Comanche cowboy figured she could see a trap before she entered it.

The ranch hands descended on the herd around midmorning. Norm led a group of riders in behind the horses to the west. Once they began driving them eastward, other groups came in on both flanks, funneling them in toward the trap. Out ahead of the herd, the mare tried desperately to find a hole through which to break out. With Blue's help and advice, though, there was always rider in place and ready to cut her back each time.

The canvas-strung fence blind to turn the herd worked, and when Blue waved a blanket over his head, guns were fired, shouts went up, the mare leaped forward, and they went down through the draw to the opening that was soon to become a closed gate.

The riders cheered. Mustanging looked too easy, but Norm knew they'd get taught new lessons before they had them all gathered. With Blue riding shotgun, though, they'd get through it without any problems.

"Kid, you made it look too easy."

Blue just inclined his head. "Be harder next time."

"Yeah, but we got a secret weapon."

"What's that?"

Norm laughed and clamped in on the shoulder. "We got *you*, boy!"

The next morning, golden sunshine swathed the low mist of rising dust from under the wild horses' hooves. Norm and Rowdy stood behind the makeshift corral, chinning the top rail.

Rowdy pointed. "That bay mare that led them, you see her?"

Norm nodded. "She's a beaut, all right."

"I think we can have some fun with her." The younger cowboy grinned. "I'd like to break her enough to race her at the dirt ranch races."

"I think she's worth a chance. Tell the boys in charge of breaking we don't want her as a cow pony, but as a racehorse."

Gunny moseyed on over from the chuckwagon, carrying a mug of coffee. "What do you two think?"

"We're going to hold that bay mare for a racehorse."

"She's fast. I bet she'd beat lots of competitors."

"Well, let's get started on today's business. We need to get some fires built. We'll cut all the stallions but the big studs we like, then brand them."

At Rowdy's direction, the ropers all saddled up to catch the colts and uncut older stallions. Fires were made to heat up irons, and the group set to work.

The pen's size made the horses hard to catch, but the veteran riders' skills brought the task to a quick conclusion. They separated out the branded stock, then ran the rest—led now by the big paint stallion—out to the gate. From there, they chased them east so they wouldn't get mixed in with another herd when they set out to catch them. Then Norm had two hands lead the fast Kentucky mare back to the ranch.

The cooking team fixed chicken-fried steaks, gravy, mashed potatoes, and some fresh green beans Edith had found in town. The day had ended with a dozen prospects of cowponies cut and branded, and one wild racing mare—as good as they could have hoped.

The next day, the outfit set out to gather and work another band of mustangs. Fifteen more possible saddlehorses were added to what they already had. When they finally returned to the ranch, they did so with sixty new animals to break.

Once they'd returned, Norm sent Rowdy off to town to buy a few wagonloads of hay. They'd need it, anyway, but with so many new horses, they'd need a good stack or two. Things were shaping up, but he couldn't turn around and not find a new expense. That was what happened when you started up a ranch, though. No sense in worrying about it.

A few of the Hispanic ranchers who had smaller herds began to deliver their yearlings for his fifteen-dollar price. Most didn't have many, but a sale of twenty head earned three hundred dollars, and with that amount they had all they needed to buy the staples they could not grow on their own for a year. The cattle were rebranded and turned out.

Rowdy's suppliers soon started delivering wagonloads of hay that had been grown down in the river bottoms. Seeing the need for their own, home-grown supply, Norm took Rowdy and Cur out looking at suitable farmable land on the ranch. The best hay was oats, which would grow during the winter warm spells, required less moisture, and made the most tonnage. They found a spread of tillable land down on the river and he ordered it fenced with wire and stays. Before another week was out, they had begun the process of clearing it of brush, then some of the hands were sent down with oxen to plow it for the next fall.

Rowdy investigated mowing machinery and stackers. He found a man who needed to sell his equipment, and they moved it to the main ranch. Then they brought in an out-of-work blacksmith, and the four of them had a hay machinery powwow.

Everett Kramer was a giant of a man and clearly knew his business. He showed them all the weaknesses in the equipment they'd bought, and how, over the winter, he could rebuild them. He could also shoe horses and fix most iron objects. Norm hired him on the spot. His wife and four kids soon joined him on the ranch—and a larger *jacal* was built for them to live in. Once they'd moved in, his wife Grace's rusty voice became a familiar sound around the homestead. The cowboys swore it could be heard for at least a half-mile in every direction. It was a good thing she and Edith got along so well.

The ranch population soon grew even larger. Cur's wife finally had her baby, a boy they called Monroe. The wives of two of the other hands gave birth that fall, as well, to two baby girls Edith couldn't help but dote over.

Edith and her three girls planned a big Christmas party. They got everyone a present and wrapped it. Cowboys got jackknives. Women got hairbrushes. Children got tops to spin and sock dolls. The weather stayed warm, and they dined outside picnic-fashion. They had lots of food, and everyone had a good time.

Norman and his foremen started making regular cattle-buying trips. Word got out when they were coming to some crossroad, and the small ranchers from the area met them there. They either contracted cattle right there, or delivered them to the Rocking Chair at a later date. Most of his buys were forty or less, but it added up. The number of head bought or pledged kept climbing. Norm began to feel more certain he would have all the cattle he needed, and the cattle the banker Hal Brooks wanted bought would be there at the Rocking Chair by shipping time. His request to the grazing association up in the Strip for a thousand more head was approved, and he was allowed pay that fee when he got there. They kept widening their search to find more young cattle to fill their needs.

THREE HISPANIC MEN rode in to headquarters one day. They wore fine suits and rode prize horses. They introduced themselves as the Vasquez brothers—Mateo, Rufus, and Carlos—and told him they came from Mexico.

Mateo led the conversation at the dining table. "We have vast cattle herds below the border. We understand you have pasture rented in the Cherokee Strip to fatten up a large herd."

"That's right. I'm buying cattle for that purpose."

"How many more can you use?"

"Eight hundred or so."

Mateo shared a look with his brothers. They both nodded.

"Where do you need them and when?"

"Early March, here. But I don't want some bawling calves to take north. I need yearlings. Horns two to three inches long."

"They will all be that old or older, or you can cull them."

"I'd like to come to your *hacienda* and see them. March is too late to say no."

Mateo agreed. "Could you use another thousand head?"

"You want to send another thousand head up to graze with me?"

"We would share the costs." The other man gave him a quick smile. "You would not need to pay us for the eight hundred head until you sell them, and we will go shares on the last thousand."

"Do you have the experienced help to send along with them?"

"To drive them?"

"Yes. Good cowboys are hard to find. I'd need them on the drive. And up on the Strip to keep the herd assembled."

He shook his head. "I can find you plenty of men and horses, but they would need to be led. They have never been there before."

"Leading the men is no problem at all. I'll just need to see those cattle."

"We'll be happy to have you visit. Will you be able to rent more pasture?"

Norm nodded. "I'm in a position to do that, but it needs to be done now."

The brothers agreed.

"That's why we came here. When can you look at our cattle?"

"Next week. I can drive down there. If we can agree, then we'll go up north as two herds in March. That would be easier to handle. I have the leaders, and they can get us there. We need a good season's graze to get them fat before we sell them in Kansas."

"This must be a great grass country, *señor*," Carlos said.

"That might be an understatement." Norm chuckled. "The best in the world that I know about. There are thousands of acres of grass and streams to water them at."

"We are businessmen, Norman. We want to be your partners, and if we can make money—we have the cattle to stock your plans. We need an American partner. We will be proud to be that partner with you."

The meeting ended, and Edith and her house staff fed them a sumptuous dinner and put them up for the night in three of the main *casa's* guest rooms. The next day, Norm and the Vasquez brothers rode with his foremen to look over the cattle he'd already bought. Norm took the chance to point out the charateristics of the kind of cows he was looking for.

"I see what you need." Mateo nodded and showed his brothers what he and Norm were looking at. "We won't bring any less than those kind. I think we can make lots of money as partners. You make the grass buy, and we'll support you with good men and money."

"I'll come down to see you next week. If we agree then, we have enough grass here to bunch your cattle until we leave."

"The smoother we can make it, the better it will work. I understand that you have driven big steers before to Kansas?"

Norm nodded. "Many times, but I worked for the other guy in the early times. This time it is mine—and my largest."

Carlos smiled at him again. He had big, white, shiny teeth. "Your reputation is strong. I think this will be a great partnership."

They shook hands, then made plans for him and Rowdy to take a stage down to the Mexican border. A small force of Mateo's men would meet them there and bring them south to their *hacienda* in a fine carriage.

A week later in Mexico, Rowdy laughed as the coach passed under the archway gate of the *hacienda*. "This is a castle, boss man. You joined some big time operators this time."

They were shown to a great suite of rooms with a flower garden attached. Their hosts provided Rowdy with a stunning young woman to entertain him during their stay. A similar offer was made to Norm, but he politely declined. He had the only woman he ever needed in his life at home. The fine wine and excellent food he was offered, though, was a different story entirely.

A day after they arrived, they were taken out to inspect the herds, and Norm was pleased to see some good cattle. The brothers had everything... everything except a well-connected *gringo* to handle business up in the Strip.

And, by God, he could sure do that. They had business papers drawn and signed. While Norm had been a little suspicious at first, his conscience was now clear. The brothers would be a great investment. It looked like he'd lucked into some more good fortune. They agreed to bring cattle to the Texas line, dip them, and then bring them to the ranch. Herd animals that grazed together solved the first social problems, and they wouldn't spend all their time fighting when they headed further north.

So, the merger began with the cattle branded to his trail mark. The open mild winter put many pounds on all the stock.

In spite of having the new *vaqueros,* Norm still needed a couple more hands and experienced trail cooks, so he put the word out early, and riders began to trail in looking for jobs. He hired on two brothers from Fredericksburg, James and Jeremy Menefee. James had been on a Kansas drive the previous year, and Jeremy wanted to tag along this time out. Norm liked the looks of them and decided to give them a try.

A BOUT A WEEK later, an old cowboy rode in with an old packhorse trailing along behind him..

"Howdy." Norm tipped his hat to the newcomer. "Come on down and stretch your legs. You can water your horses at the trough."

"'Preciate it," said the old-timer. "I'm looking for work. Name's Bob Cook."

"Well, Mister Cook, I'm hiring hands, but this is going to be a tough drive, and to be fair—"

"I understand that you want younger fellas to drive cattle. I did that myself when I was younger. I heard you might need a cook."

"I do. Tell you what, Bob. You put your horses in the corral, spend the night in the bunkhouse. The chuckwagon is there by the barn, and it's stocked. You fix breakfast for the boys, and we'll see what they say. Fair enough?"

"Sounds fine to me, Mister Thompson."

"All right, then. Call me Norm."

"I will, if you'll call me Cookie." The old man gave him a crooked smile.

"Okay, Cookie. Whatever you like."

Norm told Edith about Cookie and said he was going to have breakfast with the hands in the morning so he could make a good judgement.

"I think that's a fine idea. Mind if I join you?"

"Why, Missus Thompson, I think that would be fine, just fine."

They awakened next morning to the sound of a triangle ringing. When they stepped out on the porch, there was a line of cowboys at the back of the chuckwagon, a fire ring with two coffee pots going, and everyone seemed to be in good humor.

They walked over and found Cookie smiling and serving up heaping plates of pancakes, molasses, bacon, biscuits, and a simmering pot of beans for those who preferred it. As they heaped their plates full, Cookie said, "Save some room." He pulled back the cotton cover on a huge pan of doughnuts. The aroma of cinnamon filled the air around him.

Norm glanced at Edith, who nodded her approval.

"Looks like you've got yourself a job, Cookie."

"All right!" Cookie rubbed his hands together happily. "But your chuckwagon ain't quite stocked like I like it."

"Oh? What's missing?"

"I'd like another sack of dried apples, a box or two of raisins, and a ten-pound sack of cornmeal."

"Okay, then. I'll pick 'em up next time we go to town."

"Also, I prefer to cook with my own pots and pans. I brought them on my packhorse."

"That's fine by me. There's an empty tack box just inside the barn. Put the ones you don't need in there."

Cookie looked at Edith and laughed. "Is he always this hard to get along with, ma'am?"

Over the next few days, Norm and Cur hired six more riders. They'd need at least a dozen for the drive, and some would have to stay at the ranch with Edith. They got it done, though, and when the first signs of spring started popping up, they had two outfits ready and two *remudas.*

It was nearly time to start his big gamble.

Time to head for the Cherokee Strip.

CHAPTER No. 14

NORM'S NEW PARTNERS had brought some good horses and even better cowboys up from Mexico. His original intention had been to have Rowdy remain in charge at the ranch, things had changed. Not only had Rowdy proved himself to be invaluable to the outfit, he also spoke more Spanish than Cur, so Norm detailed him to lead the *vaqueros.* In his place, Roby Hindsman would be the stay-at-home manager of the Rocking Chair while they were gone. Cur would lead the Texas boys, and the herd was split fifty-fifty between his bunch and Rowdy's. Carlos Vasquez, the youngest of the three brothers from Mexico, came along, too. After a big sendoff, the first herd, led by Cur with Norman, left northbound. Two days later, Rowdy and Carlos took the second out the gate to follow. Storm clouds darkened the sky, but they were on their way.

The first day's thunder grumbled as they left south Texas and nosed ahead. Individually, steer after steer broke to go back, but in three days, they fell into a *you lead, and I'm coming right behind you* mindset.

They lost their first man on the fourth day. Alfred Charles was the youngest drover with the herd, and this was his first cattle drive—first time away from home, for that matter. Being a kid, he was assigned to ride drag, chasing the steers along just by keeping pressure on them to get out of the way. Skirting a large clump of Texas mesquite, his horse shied, and he lost his seat. He landed on his hip and had the wind knocked out of him. As he started to roll over and get up, though, he found himself face-to-face with the rattler that had caused his horse to shy. He might have still been okay if he'd remained perfectly still and waited it out, but he was young and green. He went for his gun, instead.

The rattler struck first and got him on the inside of his left thigh. Alfred managed to put two slugs in the snake before his own veins delivered the poison straight to his heart.

The shots brought Norm and two other riders at a fast gallop, but they were too late for Alfred. Norm delayed the drive for a day while they did what they could for him, but he was gone the next morning. They buried him on a South Texas hillside, said some words over him, and pushed on north.

Six to eight miles a day was plenty, and these cattle had been herded a lot, which made them much better to work. The first Texas cattle ever driven north had been in the brush all their lives and were deer-like at any chance to break and run.

They crossed the Colorado without losing a man or a cow, but Harry Ikeman's horse stepped in a hole, and he got soaked to the skin. To make matters worse, a bad thunderstorm caught them on the other side. They spotted a small tornado off to the northeast, but all they got was strong winds, torrential rain, and hail.

The steers rolled their eyes and clacked their horns together as they milled about, refusing to bed down. Every man rode night herd to keep them from stampeding. Norm had Cookie keep coffee hot for them all night and allowed them to ride in for a cup one at a time. By morning, everyone's nerves were frayed, and they were bone tired.

When the storm ended, Norm passed the word that they'd hold the herd there and rest for a day before moving on. The grass was good. There were feeder streams to the Colorado for the cattle and horses to water in, and one day wouldn't make much difference.

By afternoon, Harry Ikeman had a high fever, chills, and kept coughing like he couldn't get his breath. They got him out of his wet clothes, dried him off, and bundled him up the best they could. Norm had the boys make a place for him in the supply wagon before they headed out the next day.

"How's Harry doing?" Norm asked Cookie when they stopped for a noon break of coffee and jerky.

"No improvement, boss. He's still coughing quite a bit and seems feverish."

"See if you can't get some broth in him. He's got to hang on. Nearest town is Waco, and it'll be near a week to get there. They'll have a doctor for him."

Everyone pitched in doing what they could to keep him warm and try to cheer him up, but by the third day, he was coughing up blood.

"Purty sure it's pneumonia," Cookie whispered to Norm when he came around checking again. "It don't look good."

"Has he taken any broth today?"

"Not a thing since yesterday afternoon and not much then."

"You got any ideas what we can do for him?"

"Not a one except what we're doing. Keep him warm. Try to get him to take liquids."

"All right. Keep at it. If you need to stop—stop. I'll have the drag riders keep an eye out and let me know if you do."

It was pretty glum around the campfire that night. Harry was well-liked, but the hands mostly kept their thoughts to themselves as they rolled into their blankets and tried to sleep.

Norm woke up to Harry's coughing around four in the morning. He rolled out and went to check in on his condition. Cookie was sitting up with him and shook his head when he saw Norm.

"He's coughing up something gray now. Maybe part of his lungs. He hasn't got long."

"Is he conscious?"

"In and out, but mostly out now."

Norm climbed up in the wagon and took Harry's hand. He lay perfectly still except for when a coughing spasm shook him. It was first light when he opened his eyes and looked around.

Norm leaned down to ask if he could eat something.

Harry weakly shook his head. "So long, boss," he said and was still.

Norm continued to hold his hand until he could get his feelings under control, then he gently laid Harry's hand on his chest and closed his eyelids for the last time. He took a deep breath, letting it out slowly and shook his head to clear it before climbing out of the wagon.

The men were gathered for breakfast and all looked up expectantly. He slowly shook his head.

"Gawdammit!" said one of the men who had ridden with Harry for a couple of years. "Gawdammit to hell, anyway."

Before noon, yet another crude cross marked their trail north.

New grass sprung up under the warming sun, and four thousand head trampled north toward the Cherokee Strip for a summer of grazing to fatten them and then off to the feed yards or slaughter.

Spring rains fattened the murky rivers, and every crossing possessed its own hazards. The Brazos was running bank full, and they had to wait three days for it to recede enough to cross. Even then it wasn't easy. Though Both herds had veteran lead bell-steers that struck for the north bank, swirls, currents, and whole uprooted trees going downstream made the swim for the far side hazardous. Norm sent up a rare and silent prayer when they all made it across safely.

Two days north of the Brazos crossing, Cabe Forrest's horse stepped in a prairie dog hole while he was chasing a break-away steer. Cabe took a header and broke his arm in the fall. The horse broke its leg and had to be put down.

Cookie and Norm set Cabe's arm and put it in a splint, then made a sling for it to rest in while it healed. Cabe insisted he could still ride, so Norm put him on flank and asked one of the other flankers to keep an eye on him. He sent Gunny after the wayward steer and went to tell the point men to start looking for a good bedground for the night.

He'd no sooner reached the head of the herd when he heard a gunshot. Riding back, he saw a man come walking over a slight rise carrying his saddle. It was Gunny.

"What in hell happened?"

"That blamed steer turned back and ran right through that prairie dog town again. By the time I saw what he'd done, it was too late. My horse stepped in a hole and broke his right foreleg."

"That steer ain't worth two horses, let alone a good man. If he comes out of there, shoot him, and we'll give him to Cookie. I ain't risking another man nor horse on his worthless hide."

They'd already lost a cowboy to a rattlesnake bite and another to pneumonia. One had a broken arm from being tossed from a bronc but was healing. Two horses involved in wrecks had to be destroyed. Bad as it was, Norm was glad there was nothing worse. Such things were simply part of the day in, day out life of trailing cattle north.

Carlos and Norm met to go over things before they crossed the Red River and entered the Indian Territory. The man was in his twenties and had a wife, Rosa, and three children who were staying back at Rocking Chair keeping Edith company while they were gone.

They sat on a high point watching the snaking line of steers going north.

"You enjoy this?" Carlos asked.

"Oh, yes, we're moving good. The grass has really grown this spring. Some years it stays cold too long. We been lucky. The rivers to cross have not been real bad, and I think these younger cattle drive easier than older ones. But we had them mixed before we started out, and they were more used to each other—it all helped."

"You like our partnership?"

"Absolutely. We can all make more money. I don't owe as much money this way, which is better."

"I have written my brothers that you have been very open with me, and we work well together. Your men treat my *vaqueros* very politely and as their equals. I am certain, if anyone threatened your men, they would ride to help them."

"Same here. Is your wife liking the ranch?"

"Yes. She thinks your wife is a nice lady who treats her well."

"This is a big move for us, but I think you'll agree when you see the grass up there and how well cattle do on it."

"We didn't know how you would accept us, but I am grateful. We needed each other. We knew we needed an American partner to make this move. People said you were an hombre to ride the river with and not out to skin everyone that you do business with."

Norm chuckled. "Last summer, I was just a foreman looking for work when my luck turned. I knew if I could find the cattle, I could make money on the Strip. Things fell into place is all I can say."

"What will you do next?"

"If this works, I'll bring more back next year and build my cow numbers at home."

"Maybe we can partner more, huh?"

"Yeah, we might well do that. You have good men, good cattle, and we'll make this summer work."

They shook hands and went back to moving their cattle.

Blue, Cur, and Norm rode north the next day and surveyed the country. There was lots of grass, and they planned to slow down the distance each day to get more gain on the cattle. They'd soon be in the Strip country, and he'd need to ride on to the Grazing Office headquarters in Baxter Springs, Kansas, to settle with them.

Cur sent two of his men to ride with him. Phil Doone and Prairie McCarty were mounted and ready to ride with their bedrolls strapped on behind them. Their horses acted a little spooked, but none of them did much more than bob their heads. Rifles at the ready in their scabbards, they were Kansas-bound in the cool morning air. Only a few scattered clouds dotted the open skies, but the mud tracks of the trail were sloppy, so they rode in the grass except where they were forced by brush or woods to use the road ruts.

"Ain't no damn highway," Prairie said.

"Just so we get there some time," Norm said.

"If we weren't so early, this whole area would all be a bigger mud bath. We got up here early and got lots of great fresh grass for them steers, but this road will be beaten down shortly by thousands of hooves into a muddy slop yard."

"That many coming?" Norm asked.

"Hell, yes. Every Tom, Dick, and Harry will be making swings to keep them rolling."

"We're lucky we get to stay up here all summer," Phil said.

"You might get lucky and find a purty woman like the boss found last year."

"She'd probably be uglier than a billy-goat and have such buckteeth she could eat grass through a picket fence."

"He must have rode a thousand more miles to find her. I never seen one that nice-looking in ten trips north. No, sir, there ain't no good-looking gals like that running around up here."

"Aw, hell, Prairie, you just ain't been looking."

"Buddy, let me tell ya—I bet I been in more tents looking for the right one than you can count."

Norm never said a word. He'd not been in many tents in his time, but he'd looked, too, and most of those women he found were either ugly or married to someone else. He heard once there was only one female in the west for every seven men. The last place he expected to find one was where he found her—things had a strange way of working out. No one knew anything about her, which suited him fine. She wasn't brassy like he imagined most of them were, and he felt lucky. He'd be glad when the long session for the grazing was over, and he was back in Texas with her. Maybe the next season, his men could run the grazing operation, they'd all have the year's experience under their belts. Meanwhile, they moved north at a steady pace with little trouble. Maybe, too damn good. He had checked twice on the second herd in the past ten days.

Rowdy and Carlos and the *vaqueros* made a good outfit. In a short while they would be able to pick out a spot to place their headquarters. He might learn where they wanted him to settle for the summer when he paid the rest of the grazing fee payment.

He knew one thing, though—it would be a long summer without Edith.

That night, he had two bad dreams. In one, the big Rocking Chair house burned to the ground, and in the other, he was standing in a small church house graveyard, and his wife's name was chiseled on a fine granite monument—*EDITH.*

Damn.

CHAPTER No. 15

H E MET WITH the man in charge of grazing rent in his Baxter Springs office. The Association had bought a large store for their headquarters, but they hadn't moved into it yet. Glen Grubs was a short man, wore boots, no necktie, and he remembered Norm from the past fall.

"Thompson, did your lovely wife come back with you?"

"No, sir. She's going to have a baby. It'll be our first, and we decided she better stay close to the house in Texas."

"Well, she is sure a beautiful woman. I hope you two have the best of luck with the baby business. I was looking forward to meeting her again. I received the bank drafts from your banks. One from Clermont in the Indian Territory, and the other from San Antonio."

"Good. That's why I came by to see you, to show you that we were acting in good faith. I'm above the Cimarron River, east of the western cattle trails to Dodge. I haven't seen any cattle in the area."

Grubs took him to a large map on the wall, and Norm used a pointer to show where they were camped.

The Association man rubbed his chin and nodded. "If this area is satisfactory to you, then you're free to stay there. You're allowed to build some shelters and traps if you need them, of course, but be warned, they'll become our property if you do not return. Please bury your trash and leave the land as you found it to the best of your ability. Our protection men will try to keep outlaws from harming you, but the Strip is way too vast to cover all the troublemakers. We'll also need your help with something else. Some people come to graze here who haven't paid us to do so. If you see anyone like that, you're required to report it, along with any other outlaw activities."

"I understand. If that's all, I'll sign the papers, and get back to my herd."

An assistant took him to a desk, and Norm read the papers. They were legal papers, and he wished his wife was there to help him understand the language, but he read them and grasped the purpose. They were renting pasture, and they held the Strip as it was rented from the Cherokee tribe. The papers were signed, and the money paid to the Association for the right to graze. Too much money and effort was already spent to get there to do any more but settle in, holding the cattle on the land—and pray like hell that they got fat before frost came.

He and his men had some beer with a meal in a bar. He bought some whiskey to take back for medicinal purposes, wrapped the bottles in Turkish towels, and packed them to go back in panniers. Before dawn, they rode south for the camp, whiskey and all, on the packhorses.

Phil and Prairie gave him some guff on the way back about the U.S. Marshals arresting him for bootlegging. He laughed it off, but wanted the liquor on hand to treat anyone injured and in pain. If they were stopped, he'd explain his problem and promise they'd not let any Indians drink it. No one stopped them, though, and once in camp, they hid the liquor for use when they needed it.

He talked things over with Cur, Carlos, and Rowdy. They were pleased with the water supply in this area, as well as the spring source that boiled out in the camp. They built horse corrals and supply shelters. Cattle had begun to move out to graze. Men were assigned areas and rode out to see where they should stop and turn back cattle.

Showers came and went. A few even turned violent and some small tornadoes danced beyond them across the rolling landscape. But it was obvious to Norm how the cattle quickly filled out, and in a few weeks, they were licking their glossy hides and making swirls with their tongues. They were really fattening up on the profusion of nutritious graze.

He and Carlos made several long-range surveys to see how far the livestock had gone and how they were doing overall.

The younger man was obviously impressed by the power of the bluestem grass. "Norman, I never saw cattle do this good simply eating grass. This is real cattle country, isn't it?"

"I knew it was good, but even I'm surprised by how fast they're all fattening up."

Carlos grinned. "I wonder if my brothers will even believe my letters."

"I know what you mean, this is really great cow country now that the buffalo are gone."

"You know, I never saw a buffalo except mounted heads."

Norm nodded. "There were still a few small herds when I first came up here. But before then, there were millions ran up and down this region clear to the Rockies. I thought they were spooky, and when blocked, they got mad—like fighting bulls."

"Did you ever shoot one?"

"No. I either worked for others or had my own outfit to keep moving. I had no real reason to kill one."

"Rowdy said you once arrested some bad outlaws north of here?"

"I wasn't looking for them. I was looking for work up there coming down from Montana, and I found some mean bastard who was beating on a woman. I stepped in and stopped him. I knocked him on his butt when he fought me. He turned out to be a wanted outlaw. Then I happened on his gang planning his escape, they drew their guns, and I beat them to it."

"He also told me you were held up going home from a big drive a few years ago and shot it out with some other outlaws."

Norm gave Carlos a grin. "Yup. Buck naked, too. But someone had to do something. They'd strip-searched me for the cattle sales money I didn't have. They turned their back on me to threaten the others. I didn't even draw my gun out of the holster. I fired it still in the leather."

Carlos whistled. "You know how to take care of yourself, *señor.* Do you expect trouble out here?"

"I hope not, but there ain't much law in these parts, so any outlaws can pretty much ride around free and clear. You see, once in while a couple U.S. Marshals ride by looking for whiskey and wanted men. But it's a vast land, hundreds of miles long and wide. Too much to police."

"Will it get hot as the days get longer?"

"Oh, yes. You, living south of Texas, have less change in the day's length. In Montana we had long summer days and short winter ones."

"Rowdy said you hated the winters up there?"

"It gets too damn cold."

"Lots of snow and ice?"

"Plenty. Too much." Norm turned, his smile vanishing. "I smell smoke on the wind."

Carlos squinted from under his Stetson hat in the midday glare. "I do, too."

"We'd best ride in that direction."

A half-mile south of the first whiff in his nose, Norm and Carlos rode over a hill and saw the source. Some hipshot horses, a campfire, and some men around it cooking something.

"Keep your wits about you. I mean be ready. They look tough."

"They already have their hands on their gun butts."

What could they be doing here in no-man's land? Six tough men in an isolated area? Nothing good. "I see that. Unlikely to be ordinary folks."

Carlos nodded as they approached the hard-eyed, bearded men in shabby clothes. Their horses had been ridden hard and put up sweaty.

"Howdy."

One of the taller men spit tobacco aside and stepped out. "I know you ain't a damn marshal riding with that greaser. What's your gawdamn business up here?"

"Cattle. I'm leasing this land. Carlos and I are partners, and I don't appreciate you calling him that. What's *your* business up here?"

"I don't give a damn what you like. For two cents I'd'a shot your gawdamn head off, mister."

"You've got a gun." Norm checked his horse and gave him a nod. "Try it and see what happens."

"What's your damn name?"

"Norman Thompson. I get my mail at Baxter Springs, Kansas, and live down by Kerrville, Texas, when I'm home. What's yours?"

"Joe Smith."

A smile cut through Norm's mouth. This guy didn't dare buck him in a draw. He was a tough talker with no backbone. "That ain't what your mother called you."

"Screw you, mister." The man turned away to ignore him.

"I'll tell that U.S. Marshal I talked to yesterday where he can find you."

The man looked back over his shoulder with a sneer. "Yeah, you do that."

"Come on, Carlos, this bunch is going to be moving on shortly."

Carlos backed his horse up some before they both whirled them around and headed for the ridge. Out of range, Norm motioned to him to set his horse down. When they turned to look back, a grin crossed Norm's lips. "Well, look at that. They're loading up."

"You knew that bastard was going to back down from a gunfight, didn't you?"

"Talked big, but he wanted no part of a shootout. He only shoots unarmed men in the back, by my calculations."

"They're about saddled up."

"I'll describe them to the next marshal we meet. He can talk to them."

"I'll bet they won't be close to here, then."

Norm laughed. "I bet they're some famous outlaw gang. Shame we didn't know their real names."

Carlos agreed, and they rode on back to camp.

Rowdy met them. One of the foremen stayed in camp each day, the other one rode with different hands. "Jason, put up their horses. How did the day go?"

"We found a band of merry outlaws camped south of here."

"Who were they?"

"Joe Smith, the one guy said his name was. Tough-acting smart mouth."

"Figure they're any problem?"

Norm shook his head. "I think they rode on after we left, but they were a grimy bunch."

Carlos laughed in agreement. "I thought they would go for their guns when we spotted them."

"Lots of outlaws in this country and not much law."

"That's right. But no problems today, and that's the way I like it."

"Amen," Rowdy added.

So, their days passed, his men in the saddle pushing cattle back from wandering too far from the camp. Riders passed through. Some out of work and looking, others just drifting. Norm thought some were no doubt wanted. But with his duties as headman, he had no time to go look at wanted poster faces. The two camp cooks fed them, and they rode on.

One mid-afternoon, two of their cowboys came busting in on sweaty horses. They made such a commotion, Norm put down his pen on the letter he was writing to Edith and ran out of his tent to see what was wrong. The two riders, Frank Cobb and Little Billy Ryan, booted their hard-breathing horses over toward him.

"Hey, boss, two sneaking bastards tried to rob Little Bill and me today. They had on flour sack masks and rode out of a brushy draw down there. Well, they were about to rob us, and I could tell they couldn't see good behind those masks. So, I drew my gun and shot one and missed the other before he cut out."

"Did you know the one you shot?"

Billy shook his head, dismounted, and tugged his pants out of his crotch. "Naw, we never seed them before. They was stinky dirty and looked like they'd been starving."

"Why would they try to rob you two?" Norm laughed at the notion that they expected two ranch hands to have any money worth anything.

Frank grinned. "They damn sure picked on the poorest guys in your outfit to rob."

"Cur," Norm said to the foreman who had joined them. "These Indian Territory outlaws are robbing our hands now."

"What for? Tobaccy?"

"I guess. Send some boys back and bury him. Try to catch his horse. We might learn something about him from that. Search him good for letters and that stuff. It don't have to be a fancy burial." He turned to another of his men. "Frank, get a fresh horse. One of you two to take the burial crew down there is enough. I'll go get the men to help you bury him."

Norm shook his head. What was going to happen next? Which one of his lead men told Edith, back in Texas, cattle herding was boring? Probably Rowdy. He was out with some hands. He'd tell him when he got back.

At least one good thing happened that day—Howard Kimes brought in two fat wild turkeys he shot for the camp cooks. Be something besides beef and venison in their diet. He went back to his tent to finish his letter to Edith and tell her about the great cowboy robbery attempt.

The next day, he rode back into town. Baxter Springs was a busy place. He and Cur put their horses up at the livery. They washed down the free lunch at the Wild Horse Saloon with some beer and talked to a few other men from grazing outfits. Norm planned to talk to the director in the Grazing Association Office, and Cur wanted to buy something for his wife at home and send it to her. They planned to eat supper together in the hotel restaurant that evening.

His buddy, Ike Andrews, showed up about then, and Norm went back inside the office with him to talk.

"How's your lovely wife?"

"Edith's back in Texas having our baby. It should happen sometime while I'm gone."

"Damn, she didn't look like that when I met her."

Norm smiled. "She was then."

"You're a lucky fellow. I wish I had as pretty a wife as you have."

"Ike, you don't find pretty wives in brothels."

"Guess you're right. Hey, I saw you had two herds up here this summer."

"I picked up two partners. One's a banker down in Clermont I met going home, and the others are some big ranchers in Mexico who had no good markets for their cattle. There are three brothers, and I've been to their fancy hacienda. They're big operators, but they needed a *gringo* partner."

"You really have been moving your boots."

"And I have the Rocking Chair Ranch on the Guadalupe River as well."

Ike whistled. "That's a helluva ranch. Ain't any grass growing under your boots. Hell, I thought you were doing good as a bounty hunter last year. Good thing I met you when you were still struggling, before you were a big-time ranch owner."

"The day I went to see the place there was pigeons roosting in the up-stairs of that big house."

Ike laughed. "What else?"

"The bank hired some day-workers to round up everything and auction them off to help make up their losses. We worked all fall, and we have over five hundred head they left behind."

"Holy cow. Yeah, I've been in those deals. Those hands they hired didn't know the place or give a damn. It paid the same money not to worry what kind of a job they did, they'd still get a buck a day."

"There were some bad times, too. We hung two teenage rustlers. They'd marked up about thirty calves."

"It wasn't easy, then."

"No, it was not—we knew they were only boys. Hangings are a sad busi-ness, but we had no real choice."

"All told, it's gone well, though?"

Norm nodded. "Someday it'll be a real ranch. Edith loves it, and we'll have a young'un when I get home this fall."

"You going to try it again next year?"

"I imagine I will." Norm grinned. "Hey, Ike, where's your camp at? If I get time, I'd drop by, and we could spin some yarns, huh?"

"Due south and west at the road forks. Love to see you again, like always. Remember when that big gray the old man rode on threw him off?"

"Knocked the wind out of him. I figured it killed him."

"Not that tough old man. I reckon we'll be just like him when we're gray-headed and get bucked off, grouchy as all get out."

They shook hands and parted. Norm mailed his letters at the post office and got all the mail in a tow sack for his outfits. He found two from Edith and thought there might be more.

Back at the hotel, Cur hadn't gotten back from his deals, so Norm sat down on the bed to read Edith's letters.

Dear Norm,

The baby is getting bigger every day. That boy kicks me inside like your bay horse you got from those outlaws. My, I really miss you. I hope you are eating right and doing well. The distance between us seems like a million miles. I think about the killdeer and meadowlarks that accompanied us up there.

Be very careful. I miss and love you so much. Your man, Roby Hindman, you left in charge is a very hard worker. They put out the new bulls last week. There were six Durham Shorthorns and eight white-faced Hereford bulls in the delivery. Very impressive bulls and very tame. Next year, your calf crop will be super, and I paid Mr. Van Dore exactly as the contract stated.

Love,
Edith

He had a real winner of a wife. Her and the new baby doing fine—that would be the whipped cream on the cake for him. There was a letter included for Cur from his new wife that he'd bet Edith wrote for her. No way that little Mexican girl had enough education to write a letter. But Edith was that kind of a person.

Cur came back, and they went to supper. He told him he saw his old buddy, Ike, and how the people in his area decided to bring their own. So, he was down in numbers, but already one outfit quit and went home to Texas. So, he'd have more cattle at the end. Norm never could figure how people with no experience at all thought they could do such jobs and undertook them like there was nothing to it.

In the morning they went back to the camp. The Allen Mercantile would deliver by their wagon all the things they needed on his list right to their camp in a week. Saved them unloading a chuck wagon, or worse, having to fetch it themselves. The Allen's acted like they appreciated his business, too.

Back in his own tent and his horse put up, he took a nap.

CHAPTER No. 16

BAXTER SPRINGS, KANSAS was still a wild cow town. Kansas was supposed to be dry, but no one there knew it. As rough, tough, and rowdy as the crowd assembled was, there wasn't anyone who'd try to enforce it

The Grazing Association office was still in the same large tent it had been in when he'd first arrived. They were still remodeling the store building they'd bought, but with little progress. Norm met Jonathan Gordon there, the man in charge of enforcing the grazing fees for the association.

A big man with a gray walrus mustache, Gordon shook his hand and welcomed him to the Strip. "So you're Norman Thompson. Heard a lot about you. I appreciate your business and you paying the fee charges. That's a big damn country down there. You don't know how many sneak their cattle in and try not to pay us. I hate cheats, and I'll bust a lot of them this summer. The price the association pays the tribe needs to be recovered from all of you grazers, or they'll go broke."

Norm nodded. "I have rustlers at home, and you have pasture cheaters up here."

"I bet half them cheaters stole the cattle they brought up here, too."

"Not much doubt about that. I'll watch for any cheating and send word."

He rode back to camp with Cur the next day, Prairie and Phil riding guard out beside them.

"How many letters did you get from your wife?" Cur asked.

"Three."

"She doing fine still?"

"She and the baby are all right."

"I bet you'd like to be there with her."

"Oh, yeah. But I also need to keep the ranch going, as well, and that takes lots of money. She understands. For the safety of the baby, she needed to stay home. I'll get back home, and we'll have our whole life together."

"Oh," Prairie snapped his fingers. "Almost forgot. We have a note for you some cowhand gave us in the saloon."

Mr. Thompson,
I have taken Ike to Baxter Springs to the doctor. Three men showed up and demanded money from him, and when he didn't pay them, they shot him twice. He's alive but barely. We shot one, and two escaped. I'll be at the Association office if you can help me.

John Bailey

He and Cur turned around and burned a path back up to Kansas. They reached the Association headquarters before dark. Hitching their horses, Norm noted a familiar Texas cowboy come out of the office at their arrival. It was Ike Andrews's foreman, John Bailey, and he looked very serious.

Norm extended his hand, and they shook. "Tell me what can I do to help you, Bailey?"

"Well, I don't have good news. Those three men rode into our camp two days ago and had an argument with Ike. Guns were drawn, and Ike was shot twice before any of us could move. My men shot one of them down, but the other two got away."

"What was the argument?"

"They claimed Ike had cheated them on another cattle deal a year ago, and they wanted more money."

"You have any names?"

"Yes. Brad Addison and Rollo Camay. The dead man was an employee of theirs, Chester Philips."

"Where did they go?"

"I guess south. I had to bring him up here. I'm not sure Ike will live. A doctor's treating him here—but you know how that goes. I'm lost."

Norm reached out and squeezed his shoulder. "John, I'll get a man, and we'll go find those two for you."

"I know you have lots of cattle up here, but you know how to handle killers better than I do. I sent word to ask you for your help since you arrested so many outlaws, but I was worried you would turn me down."

"Don't worry. I'll go find them."

"I appreciate it so much. Our camp is fifteen miles east of yours on Cherry Branch. Anyone can point us out."

"I'll go by to check on Ike, and we'll be there tomorrow."

He and Cur went by the doc's place and spoke to Ike for a few minutes. His old pard looked white as the bandages that wrapped him. He knew he was using all the energy he had to even talk to him.

"Brad's... part Injun. Eagle feathers in his hat band. Rollo... big guy. His gut hangs over his saddlehorn. Lost his right ear in a fight. Other guy—bit it off, they say... but I—I never cheated 'em—they had nothing more coming—I swear to you."

"You rest easy. Don't worry, we'll get it handled. Get well. I'll help your man later if you're still laid up. Get well."

"Thanks...."

They rode back to camp under the stars. Once there, he discussed his deal with Carlos, Cur, and Phil who'd waited up for his return. They decided in the morning that Phil would ride with him to find the shooters. Carlos said he'd manage the *vaqueros* all right until they got back.

They picked out two packhorses for them, set all they'd need out to camp, and rode out before daylight for Ike's camp over east.

They reached it by midmorning, but only by pushing the horses harder than he wanted. They rode steadily south, and a few hours later they found a fat squaw under a small canvas shade selling roasting ears of corn out of a beat-up wagon at a crossroads.

She never got up. Norm dismounted and squatted before her.

"Two?" He held up two fingers. "Two men rode by here two days ago? One had no ear." He touched his ear. "No ear. You see them go by here?"

Still deadpan, she nodded with her brown arms still folded.

"Can you tell me when?"

She nodded, but said nothing. He looked at the stack of husked corn ears in the wagon bed and sighed. "Look, you tell me where they went, I'll buy *all* your damn corn."

That got her talking.

"Hell, mister, you do that, I'll not only tell you where they're staying, I'll tell you how to get there, too." She gave him a lewd grin. "Then I'll take you behind my wagon and give you a ride that horse won't give you."

Behind him, Phil started laughing so hard he about fell off his mount trying to contain himself.

Norm bit his lip to keep his own smile at bay. "How much?"

"Ten dollars. Which one of you wants to go first?"

He handed her the money. "Ma'am, we're in a hurry to find these guys."

"They are in a shack on Little Bear Creek with two squaws. They're a couple of no-good bastards. If you gotta leave 'em for the buzzards, no one will cry about it." She got on her knees and made a map with a stick in the dust. "You follow?"

Phil dismounted and looked over her directions. "Yep. Thank you kindly."

"What is your name?"

"Norman Thompson. This is Phil Doone—one of my foremen at the Rocking Chair ranch in Kerrville, Texas."

"I am Lola Good Heart."

Norm tipped his hat. "Thank you, Lola Good Heart."

"If you change your mind about that ride, I'll be here." She winked.

Two hours later, with the sun dropping down in the west, they hitched their horses in some locust trees. Rifles in hand they approached the cabin, taking care to stay out of sight. Two Indian women were cooking over a fire in the yard. Two men sat on the low front porch taking turns drinking whiskey from a large crock. The fat one had no right ear.

They approached the back of a shed for cover and could hear them cussing at the women about something. They stepped out with their rifles ready to shoot.

"Hands up or die."

Rollo very carefully sat the crock down. The two women wrapped in blankets began to ease away.

"Stay right there," Norm ordered. Brad was standing up when all at once he broke for his pistol. A wrong move for him to try. Norman cut him down with two bullets in the chest that slammed him on his back on the porch.

"Damn it, I ain't doing a thing. Don't shoot," Rollo whined.

"You women understand English?"

Huddled together, they both nodded.

"Fix some supper." He disarmed the fat man and made him sit on the ground in the firelight. Phil went to bring their horses into the place. The two women went back to cooking.

They had some cornbread they made in a frying pan. Norm didn't like the looks of their stew. He ate a few pieces of cornbread while Phil unloaded the animals.

They handcuffed the prisoner and put him in leg irons so he could not run away. He grumbled but didn't dare say anything more, considering what had happened to his partner.

Phil tried their stew, then he settled for the cornbread too. Their prisoner ate two bowls the women fixed for him and belched a lot. Norm, meanwhile, figured he'd spend the whole night in an outhouse if he ate much of it.

Neither of the women talked much English, but Phil made some real Arbuckle's coffee, and they drank some of it and smiled a lot.

Norman took Phil aside to offer his idea on their prisoner's fate. "I have no idea if he has any reward on him. But there isn't much law enforcement out here. I say we hang him, and the world won't miss him."

"You remember the fat gal back there selling corn said no one would miss him or his buddy."

Norm had to smile at that. "I agree with her. We'll find a stout tree and do it come morning."

Phil agreed.

"We'll have to take turns guarding him tonight."

"Whatever you think best."

"This is real tough country, and only the tough will survive, won't they?"

"That sums it up. They shot Ike, and like you said, he's not a guy you rile easy. I'll plan on making a noose tomorrow morning."

"That would be a good idea."

Phil shook his head. "I would like to hear all the crimes that those two guys committed before we string him up."

"Aw, Phil, they never gave anyone a chance. It would be too bloody and mean to even listen to."

"You're probably right. I guess it will go to their grave."

Norm and he talked to the women at the fire. "I don't know who owns this place, but tomorrow you can stay or leave. They won't need the horses and things. You can have them."

Squatted in the firelight, they looked at each other and nodded.

"We go home," the thin-faced one said.

"Do that. Thank you."

They nodded.

In the morning, they had oatmeal Phil cooked for them. Then he made the noose. Norm found a stout large limb on a big walnut tree, a quarter mile away. They took the handcuffs off and tied his hands behind him. They led a horse into a ditch and loaded him on it. He was babbling about how they had him all wrong, and all the good things he did in his life, and if they'd let him go, he'd dedicate his life to Jesus.

When Phil adjusted the noose on his neck next to his left ear, he said, "You ain't going to see him where you're going."

"Oh, I swear I am saved," the man shouted, sweat dripping from his face.

"Not so far as I can see, you're not." Norm stood behind the horse with a rope coiled in his hand, shouted at the mount, and slapped him on the rump with it. The rope squeaked under his weight. His neck cracked, and he swung limp.

Phil went after the pony to bring him back to the women so they could use him to ride off. With them on their way, the two men readied the shack for a funeral for the other dead outlaw, put both bodies inside, and set it on fire after the horses were loaded.

At midday they passed the corn seller. Norm bought some of her corn for Ike's and his own camp.

"You plenty good guys," she thanked them, and they rode on.

"She didn't ask about them, if we hung them or what."

"She probably knew. Indians got ways of knowing the news you and I ain't got access to."

"She'd be nice to share a bed with in the winter. Up here in the summer, she'd be pretty hot."

"Ain't never anything good all the time, Phil."

"I had a woman nice as you have, I'd get me a job closer to home."

"She'll be fine. Having a baby and all, she's better off in Texas than up here."

"I guess so. But I couldn't leave her."

"Phil, there's lot's of things in life you have to do. Grazing these cattle up here is part of my got-to-do things."

"I see all that, but, boss man, it must be real hard on you not to have her with you."

"I'll make it. A year ago, I was stumbling around Nebraska looking for work. Then I got in a scrape with an outlaw and found her. Things went to getting better by the day. We'll have our lives to live out on that big ranch with kids to raise and cattle of our own to tend."

"How many summers will you spend up here?"

"Now I got you and Cur trained? I dunno. As long as they got grazing and I can buy cattle worth the money to raise up."

"Good. At least I got work for another year."

Norm laughed. "That long, anyway. I'm going back up to Kansas tomorrow and see about Ike. Him and I had some good times together."

"I hope he's better. Better take a hand along, After what happened to Ike, ain't no telling the bad guys drifting in and out of here."

Upon their return, they told Bailey that they'd taken care of the two outlaws that shot Ike.

Bailey spat. "No more than they deserved."

Carlos had come down to see what was happening, and with Cur and several riders, they ate a late supper and told them the shooters were no more. Nothing had happened while they were gone, and Norm and Phil rode to town to check on Ike.

Ike looked weaker and paler. The doc thought he'd make it but said it was still touch and go. His pal thanked him for coming by and said Bailey knew that he'd help him disburse the herd if he couldn't in the fall.

Before they left, they picked up the mail, and Norm was pleased to see that Edith had written to him again.

In her letter she said that the days were growing closer and his son was kicking the fire out of her. The ranch was quiet, and things were smooth. They had some beneficial rains, no storms. The grass was growing. It was hotter in Texas than she recalled, but despite her size, she was doing fine and missed him. She added a postscript. "Tell Carlos his wife is fine, and the kids enjoy swimming in the river every day."

He rode back with the mail for his men. Days passed at a snail's pace. They had a string of days with heavy thunder showers, but it didn't blow much around. Finally, in August, buyers began to come around to sign up for cattle buys.

Norm asked a man who had been coming here for a few years about how to make a good deal on them.

The man grinned. "Oh, if the price is higher, they'll be back to buy them. If the market is lower, you won't ever see them again."

"When should I sell?"

"By October fifteenth. After that you may have to stay here another year."

"That frost time?"

"Yep."

"I want to be headed home by then."

"It's the best thing to do." The man waded off toward a tent with some scantily-dressed doves waving for him to come across the street so they could treat him. Norm grinned. There might be snow on the mountain, but there was still fire in the stove. The man had to be past sixty.

Late in August, he learned in the letter that he had a son, William Norman Thompson, and he was sound and healthy and had a loud voice like his pa. She was fine, and things were well on the Guadalupe River in Texas.

September, he began talking to buyers. He found a man with a good reputation, and he had two-stage pricing. Bigger steers weighting over eight hundred he'd pay eighty-five dollar a head. Under that weight but in good flesh, he'd pay seventy-five.

He and Carlos decided that was fair, and they started moving cattle to the train yard as the buyer arranged for cattle cars.

Ike was still bedridden, and he let Norm to sell his herd the same way. So, Norm went and told Bailey to get them gathered.

Cur got crossways with another foreman about who loaded their cattle next, and they exchanged a few shots. Norm had to come to town and bail him out of jail. Things simmered down, and they got all his cattle shipped. The other two Vasquez brothers came up there to join Carlos, and Hal Brooks drove a buggy up from Clermont to celebrate their success. Since he was a banker, they had him oversee the payment. Wells Fargo was set up to dispense the money after the pasture bill and expenses were all paid.

The Vasquez brothers also had an account in a San Antonio Bank. They made around a hundred thousand dollars after the costs were taken out. Brooks made fifty thousand on his deal. After Norm paid his cowboys some good wages and paid the bank loan off, Norman had almost eighty thousand left for his part.

He made plans for four thousand head of cattle the following year. The brothers wanted the same deal, and so did Brooks.

He took a few hundred dollars out for his expenses to get home, and they headed on south. Wells Fargo, as always, handled the money. The trip took them three weeks, and he rode hard with Carlos and Phil for the last two days in his eagerness to get to the Rocking Chair ranch.

NORM FOUND A wild reunion with his wife. His son was small but loud, and the three of them danced together in an afternoon shower, then they ran for the house.

Wet, her hair plastered to her head and drying the baby with a towel, they fussed over him.

She beamed. "Bill don't mind. Isn't he good looking?"

"Yes, he's a dandy. How are you doing?"

"Glad you're home. It has been a long summer without you. But I can't believe all you have gotten done since you stood in my tent and asked me to join you."

He hugged both of them tight. "That was the greatest day of my life. I can't believe how things have changed for two nobodies."

"You aren't a nobody. You saved my life. You showed them how to take cattle to pasture, and in one year we are out of debt. Oh, Norman, I don't regret a night I missed you, but I am sure grateful you are home. How is Ike?"

"He's an invalid. I thought he'd get over it, but they took him home in a wagon. He can barely walk at all. Makes me sick. His attackers are dead, but that doesn't help him."

"Can we do anything to help him?"

"We need to think how."

"I can only say, thank you, dear God, you brought my man home."

Later that day, the whole crew crowded in the house as thundershowers began to split up and roll north.

"Thank all of you for your hard work. You did a great job keeping my wife safe and operating this ranch. We had a very successful summer in the Cherokee Strip. Thank Carlos and his family for helping our success by going up there with us. Hal Brooks, the banker who helped us in Clermont, is another man we are very grateful for. All our partners want to do it again next year.

"I saw all your hard work on the ranch you have done here. We will be sowing oats for hay on the land you've cleared and fenced and begin to store fodder for the dry years we have down here in Texas. We plan to have a great fandango to celebrate our success."

A cheer went up.

"The Rocking Chair Ranch will continue to expand. That means job security for everyone. God bless you, and thanks for bringing life back to this once great ranch."

He shook many hands, and when they left, he collapsed on a new cow-hide chair. "Is this furniture from Alan's office?"

She grinned at him. "The same craftsmen made them. I knew you'd win, and I wanted you to come home to something suitable for a big Texas rancher."

He hugged and kissed her. "This place is a long way from a soddy in Kansas, isn't it?"

"A very long way, even from a tent in Nebraska."

"Oh my, yes. We did have our first real meeting in your tent. I think we both were shaking."

"You may have been shaking. I was trembling."

"I appreciated your kindness toward me. You were who I imagined as a girl my husband would be that night. You restored my beliefs to where they were before that vicious man took my innocence beside the road in Kansas. I thought I'd never escape from his clutches." She gave him a steady look that was filled with love. "You, Norman Thompson, were a light in the darkness."

"You won't have to worry about that ever again. Let's sneak off to bed. We have lots to catch up on."

She kissed him. "Modula has Bill tonight. We can have all night."

"I'll need it."

"Yes, my dear, you will."

Damn, he was glad to be back home and holding her.

CHAPTER No. 17

HIS THREE FOREMEN met with him over breakfast. Roby Hindman, who had stayed behind and ran things, told them he bought six more bulls to be certain there was enough bull power around since most of the new ones were young.

"Good move," Norm said. "A calf born at the start of calving season is important, or we have to feed him another year to send him to market. So, shooting for an early March delivery is the way to go."

"I've heard about several sellouts coming up for cow herds," Randy said. "I have sale bills of these future auctions since we talked about increasing our herd."

Norm looked them over. "I bet this sale out west would be a good one. Says all the cows are half or more shorthorn cows. There will be an estimated five hundred pairs for this estate sale. It's in three weeks. I'll plan to attend. The sooner we get our cows to being full British breeds, the sooner we'll be a leader. Buyers, more and more, discount the longhorns."

Rowdy nodded. "Sounds good."

Roby spoke up. "Say, didn't you know old man Eakins?"

"I met him once."

"Right after you headed north, he sold off all his cows, bought a new Henry, and said he was going hunting. No one's seen him since, but every couple of weeks someone nails a Comanche scalp to the doorframe of that old cabin he lived in."

"Tough old man. Hope he's still alive." Norm shook his head. "What else?"

"We need to roundup the mustangs and sell them to a killer if we can't deal with them another way. Mustangs are a liability eating grass the cows can eat. "

"Agreed," Norm said. "Rowdy, when we get everyone settled, you'll lead that effort. I know it is not an easy thing, but we're a beef factory, and there's no place for them here. There'll always be mustangs. There simply won't be any of them on the Rocking Chair in the next eighteen months."

Everyone at the kitchen table nodded.

"We'll start back buying yearlings for next year. I want as many as we had this time out. Our partners will join us. Anything I need to know?"

No one spoke.

"Cur, start cutting the old cows and their calves, so we can market them at weaning time. If we bunch them in one area, they'll be easier to cull."

Later in the week, he and Phil went to San Antonio for the meeting with his banker. Edith stayed home with the baby again. They took a buckboard and drove in over two days travel.

Alan saw their entry as being like a victory dance in his office. The bank president came by and shook their hands, plus thanked them for their business, then left him to list his loan needs. He planned to take two thousand of his own and a thousand for the banker. Then the brothers wanted three thousand head and made an agreement to pay him ten bucks a head, or higher if they could get it.

Alan was impressed. He was certain the bank wanted to participate in the game. Once that was set up, he and Phil went back to the Alamo Square and had lunch in a hotel.

They met another rancher from the hill country, Jasper Means, and his daughter, Wanda Harold. She was a short girl, too wide to be alluring, but she missed no chance to try to charm the two men, and they shared a table for the meal with his twosome.

Norm knew some facts about her. Widowed at eighteen. Bandits had gunned down her husband during a stage robbery. After that, she had been involved with several men, married and single.

"So, you were in on his record Kansas cattle sale?" she asked Phil.

"Yes, ma'am. I was one of the foremen on the drive."

"Did you have any trouble?"

"Two masked outlaws tried robbing two of our poorest cowboys at one point, but otherwise, no."

Wanda laughed. "Really. Mister Thompson, what did you do?"

"Miss Wanda, I'm just Norm. My men shot one of them, and we never found the other one."

"They must have thought you paid them big wages, huh?"

"I think they were desperate is all. That's a big isolated land up there in the Strip."

"Did you have any close calls?"

"No. Just punched steers with them."

"Do I understand correctly that your wife had a child by herself while you were up there, Norman?"

"She decided to do that. Besides, all they'd needed me there for was to boil water."

The men laughed. She didn't, batting her eyelashes at him, instead. Norm ignored her. He could tell she wanted to move in on him, but this woman simply did not charm him at all, even if he didn't have Edith at home.

Means cleared his throat. "Are you going back?"

"Definitely."

"Father, maybe we should look into this grazing venture," Wanda said.

"There are several parts of it could be profitable. What do you credit your success in that venture to, Norman?"

"It was a good season. They got some timely rain this past season, and that helped the forage quality. But it is the old buffalo range. They thrived on it before white men came along."

"No fences, no boundaries, makes it a pretty wild country, doesn't it?"

"It takes some good hands to keep them from wandering too far. One of my friends ended up handling fifteen hundred head from three operators who told him they didn't need him and would do it themselves in the start, but he made it work, and so did we."

"It must be tough, or more would do it." Means said.

She quit arguing at that point, but Norm knew that didn't mean she'd given up. No matter, he was not taking her on as a partner, she only wanted to manipulate him into some triangle that suited her. The word was out how he had rebuilt the Rocking Chair into the one time show place of Texas of old days and put it back on top. And they did it with working people who loved working there.

He damn sure didn't need Wanda Harold. But he knew she was a determined person and spoiled by her father, and he considered her a threat to his lifestyle and the dream he had built. Last he saw, she was making sweet eyes at Phil—maybe she thought she could get to him through his ranch hand.

Wouldn't work, but Phil didn't seem to mind the attention.

As for him, it was time to get home. He picked up a few things in San Antonio he knew Edith would like, two panniers full of supplies, and turned his horse's nose toward home. He gave Phil his salary and leave to entertain himself with Wanda or whoever he wanted for a week and left the grinning foreman for the ride back to Rocking Chair.

The journey back to the ranch on the Guadalupe was quiet, nothing but the sound of the wind in the grass and the distant calling of birds. He made camp the first night in a little valley next to a stream with live water, tied his horse to a sapling cottonwood, and sat back to watch the stars come out. The next day, he'd be home. That'd give him something to dream about.

He awoke in the dead darkness to the sound of a gun being cocked.

A harsh voice came out of the night, followed by a laugh. "I told you I'd find you, you son of a bitch."

Norm started to reach for his gun, but the man said, "Don't. I'll shoot that hand off and watch you bleed to death."

"Who the hell are you?"

"I'm the man who has been trailing you for months now. The man whose brother you killed in Montana over a stallion with a lame leg."

"You came all this way for *that*?"

"All this way and further. I been following you this whole time, waiting for a time to catch you alone."

"If you followed me from Montana to Nebraska, you had plenty of opportunities before now."

The man didn't answer for a while. When he spoke, Norm could hear the smile in his voice. "Back then, I wasn't sure I could beat you in a draw. You shot me in the right shoulder, remember? I had to let that heal. Then, when you met that woman in Ogallala, I thought I'd see what you planned to do. And it came to me—it'd mean more to me to kill you after you had a lot to lose. You have a child now, don't you?"

"Yes."

"A nice ranch, lots of hands to work for you."

"Yes."

"Made a lot of money in the cattle drive, I'd guess."

"Yes. But I don't have none of it on me now, so if you're thinking of robbing me...."

He gave another harsh laugh. "I don't have no interest in robbing you. What I want is to kill you. Slowly. You've killed men yourself. I seen it. Shot some, hanged others. Those were quick ways to die." He paused. "I'm not nearly as merciful as that."

Was this it? Was he going to die in the dark, a day's ride from home, at the hands of a man whose name he didn't even know?

The only thing was to keep him talking.

"If you don't want money, what will you gain by revenge? It won't bring your brother back."

"No. But it'll still be worth it. Knowing you were hoping to be in your woman's arms tomorrow and sending you to hell instead."

Norm knew that, even in the dark, the man could see him well enough to know if he reached for his gun. Maybe he'd pay less attention to his left hand, on the side away from where the outlaw stood. He moved his fingers slowly, silently, until they encountered a rock—and he wrapped his hand around it.

He'd get one chance. If he missed, he was dead. Even if he hit the man, he might not hurt him bad enough to keep from being shot.

Norm tried to make his voice sound sad, resigned, like he'd already given up. "At least... at least tell me what your name is. Tell me who the man is who wants to kill me so bad."

"You think a condemned man would want to know the name of the hangman, huh? That's pretty funny." He snorted. "All right, Norman Thompson. I'll tell you. My name is Jesse...."

Norm rolled over and brought his left arm around in a tight circle, hurling the rock at where the man was silhouetted against the stars. There was a thud and a crunch, a scream of pain, and the outlaw's gun went off. The bullet came so close to Norm's head that he felt the wind. He continued his roll, bringing himself up onto one knee, and pulled his own gun.

The shot cut off the man's scream, and there was a crash as he fell into the grass.

After that, only the frightened whinnying of his horse and the sound of hooves as the outlaw's own animal fled into the night as fast as it could.

He wouldn't sleep anymore, but he looked up at the stars wheeling overhead and offered one more prayer of thanks. After tonight, he had a lot more to be thankful for.

THE SUN ROSE to show the sprawled figure of the man he'd killed, the outlaw who had tracked him relentlessly all the way from Montana. Sure enough, it was the brother of the man he'd shot in a saloon in Montana. The stone had struck him full in the face. One cheekbone looked smashed to hell. That alone might have been enough to kill him if the gunshot to the chest hadn't finished him off. Not even worth taking the trouble to bury.

Leave him for the buzzards.

EDITH HEARD HIM riding up just before sunset of the next day. "Edith, darling, I am glad to see you."

She threw her arms around him. "Welcome home, Norm. I hope you don't have to go again soon. We need you here." She looked up into his eyes, and a worried frown crossed her face. "You didn't have any trouble on the way back, did you?"

How had she known? Women could tell these things, he figured. But should he tell her how close he'd come to not ever arriving home, to being shot to pieces on the Texas prairie?

No reason to. The threat was over. The only thing ahead was their life together. They'd made a start here at Rocking Chair. There'd be other drives up to the Strip in other years, but for now, it was time to rest, put it out of his mind, and give his thoughts to his wife and his son.

"No, ma'am," he said, and grinned. "No trouble at all."

CALIFORNIA JONES

A SHORT STORY

CAL BLINKED HIS burning eyes, wondering if the haze of his hangover was distorting his vision. A woman stood at the foot of his bed, and she definitely was not the usual sort of female that frequented his shack in Tucson's shanty row. This particular gal wore a spotless starched dress. She was a lady, and he didn't have the faintest notion what she was doing in his place.

"California Jones?" she asked in a very cultured voice. Cal sat up straight on the bed and scowled in pained disbelief at her beauty.

"I might be Jones." With that, he scratched his left ear and then tossed aside the thin green blanket, exposing his faded red underwear.

The woman gasped and quickly turned her face away.

"That's right, you look off over there and I'll get dressed."

"You are California Jones?"

Who in the cat hair did she think he was? Wyatt Earp? He nodded in admission as he pulled on his waist overalls, then he realized she was not looking at him and spoke up in a gruff voice. "That's my name. What's yours lady?"

"Colleen Swain."

He wrinkled his nose at the sour smelling shirt he picked off the nail on the wall. Never heard of her before. He frowned and silently repeated her name to himself as if to draw recognition from some recesses of his foggy brain. It still meant nothing to him.

"Don't reckon we've ever met," he said as he shoved his arms into the shirt. "You can turn around now," he said, primed for her next move. "If you come to preach for my soul, save your breath, sister. Better men than you have tried before. I don't give to needy causes either because I ain't got nothing, and besides, I like my way of life and ain't fixing to change."

She raised her chin up. "I have come here on business."

"What kinda business?" he asked, taken back.

"I've come to hire you."

"I don't take care of no lawns and gardens. Go two doors down. That old Messikin, Jesus Juarez, he'll help you." He pointed in that direction, but she stood unwavering, and he began to wonder what her real purpose was in being there.

"The Apaches have taken my son. I want him back." She finished and chewed on her lower lip. Close to tears, she wrung her hands to control herself as she waited for his reply.

He shook his head slowly. "If the Apaches got your boy, you need the law or the Army, ma'am, not me."

"But they've searched or so they tell me." Her blue eyes began to flood. She turned away and dabbed at them with a small handkerchief. "My Teddy is out there, Mister Jones, and they haven't found a sign of him." She drew up her shoulders and turned to face him again. "They say you can do things with the renegades."

He felt her stare. There was a time he could have helped.

Sunshine streamed in the dirt-streaked windows, illuminating her fine features. She looked to him like a gold nugget in a pile of debris. He dropped his head in defeat. "You've come to the wrong place for that kinda help."

He squeezed his eyes to shut out the pounding at his temples. His tongue felt too thick for his mouth—he needed a drink. Why didn't she leave? He'd done told her he couldn't help her. She wanted to pin him down. He avoided looking at her as the cot protested his sitting down on it.

"Go see the military." He stared at the floor for strength to tell her. "Look at me, lady. I'm nothing like the man you want." His coughing began, and it grew deeper until he bent over, fearing he would not stop until all his air was gone.

He waved her help away. Finally half strangled but regaining his breath, he looked up at the knock on the door. Who else was coming?

Before he could rise to answer it, Gladys Newton, his neighbor and drinking partner burst in. Gladys stopped at the sight of Mrs. Swain and clasped her hand to her mouth.

"Hell, Cal. Why, excuse me?" Her paunchy figure blocking the doorway, she acted undecided whether to come in or not. She drew in a deep breath, exposing a generous portion of her large bosom in the low-cut dress. "I didn't realize you had company."

"This here's Mrs. Swain. But she's leaving," he said with a wave of his hand. "But you could have saved yourself a trip. Ain't a drop of anything to drink left in this house."

With some effort, Gladys came inside and looked at the stranger. "Nice to meetcha, ma'am." At that point, she kind of curtsied as much as her fat legs would bend. "Any friend of Cal's is a friend of mine."

"Yes, er—nice to meet you too, Gladys."

"By gad, Jonesy," Gladys said with a knowing chuckle and a wink at him, "You got yourself a real looker this time. I better get back over there. And let you two get on with—ah, your business, huh?"

"Go on, Gladys," he said in disapproval as she lumbered out the door laughing like a hyena. "Don't mind her, ma'am, she don't mean no harm."

"I guess you can see, I'm not easily put off, Mister Jones," Colleen said, with a deep swallow to punctuate her sentence. "I want you to bring my son back to me."

Cal sighed aloud. Why did this stubborn woman persist to torment him? "Lady, if them Apaches did take him, and I'm saying this because you need to know, he more than likely is dead by now—"

She gave him a short nod to continue. She was tough, he decided, but she better realize the chances that boy was dead were ten times more likely than finding him alive.

"Why, I don't even have a horse or anything."

She pounced like a mountain lion on his excuse. "You can use my late husband's things. I'll get you any supplies you need."

Cal knew he was licked. She would never leave until she'd badgered him into going on this wild goose chase. "I should have figured you was a widow woman coming here all alone and all."

"Yes. My husband was killed when they took Teddy captive."

Cal recalled something about a businessman getting murdered down on the San Pedro and the son being taken off by the raiders. He scratched the thin hair on top his head, trying to recall how long ago he'd heard of the raid.

"They say you know these people. That you once lived with them."

He nodded. "Some. I scouted and rode with them, but it was a long time ago."

"You're my last hope." She wet her lips and drew her shoulders back. "And if he—Teddy—is not alive then I want to know that, too." Then she shook her head so slightly. "It is the not knowing that is so hard."

He couldn't stand to watch her any longer. He dropped his gaze to the floor. What could it hurt? Besides, he was flat broke and she would pay him to go search. He knew some camps in the mountains. But they were many miles from Tucson. Could he even ride that far? What the hell? When he got back, he and Gladys would drink the money up and rejoice.

"Where's your place?" he asked.

"Then you'll take the job?"

"Hold on here." He held up both hands to settle her down. "I'll ride out in the hills and ask some Injuns I know. They may or may not have heard of this boy. He may be in Old Mexico by now." He wanted to be certain she understood he might come back empty handed.

"I understand, Mister Jones. I just know you will find Teddy."

"Where do you live?"

"Oh, yes. Down on Fifth Street, third house on the right from the corner of Congress."

"I'll find you. Give me a quarter."

Colleen frowned at his outstretched hand. "What ever for?"

"I need a bath and a haircut, lady. I smell too bad to stay sober for long."

Without hesitation, she withdrew two quarters from her reticule and placed them in his hand.

He closed his fist over the coins. "Thanks."

"I'll be along in an hour or so. Have someone saddle that horse, put some grub in a sack, couple small sacks of corn, too and fill a couple of canteens with water." He scratched his right ear. Something inside it was itching like Hell. "I'll need a rifle and some shells." He rose and walked her to the door, still deeply engrossed in his needs.

"I'll have it all ready. Will you need money to trade for him?"

"Money? No. Let's see, I'll need four or five bottle of whisky. That should do it." He looked directly into her eyes, expecting to hear a protest at his demand for liquor. To his surprise, she quickly withdrew some bills from her purse and handed them to him.

"You'll have to buy it." She apologized, and then she started for the rig parked at his fallen down yard gate.

"Ma'am," he called out to her. "Try not to worry yourself sick. If he's alive and in the country, mind you, I'll try to find him. Worrying won't help a thing."

She turned back, dabbing at her eyes, and forced a nod in gratitude. "Thank you, Mister Jones."

Two hours later smelling like a Chinese laundry in his clean clothes and bathed, he arrived at her front door. He had allowed himself two short beers, which entitled him to a free boiled egg lunch at McCarthy's Saloon. On her front step, he belched loud enough to wake the dead, then rapped on her door. In the time between their meeting and his recovery, he had grown more doubtful about the boy's chances of being alive, but decided not to go over that with her again. She knew the risks—he certainly wasn't God.

"Oh, Mister Jones, you've kept your word." She stepped back to invite him in.

"You figure I'd light out on some drunk?" he demanded.

"There were folks said—"

"Listen, I been keeping my word all my life. That's beside the point, is that horse saddled?" He followed her into the spacious living room.

"Yes, he's ready out back."

"I hope we can wrap this whisky better, so it makes the ride." He showed her the poke he carried.

"I have some towels."

"Sounds awfully good to use for that." He looked around her fine house and felt helpless at what else to wrap the glass bottles with.

"No, they would work." She rushed off to get some. A maid returned with her, and they made quick work of wrapping the half dozen bottles of golden liquor. He didn't want to even look at the whisky as they tied the Turkish towels with string at the neck of each quart. Damn, he needed a drink—powerfully bad. His molars nearly floated away thinking how good the rye would taste flowing down his throat. He used his index finger to pry some breathing room between his neck and the stiff collar.

"There, Mister Jones, they should ride that way," she said proudly as she repacked them in the cotton sack he intended to hang from the saddle horn.

He took the bag and then looked hard at the tile floor. "I don't want you to get your hopes all up. I may not find a thing out there."

Colleen shook her head violently. "I will not give up hope. My son is alive out there. I know it!"

"All right, Mrs. Swain." He followed her through the house, not satisfied that her intuition was right.

He rode out of Tucson on the powerful sorrel horse, the whisky bottles in the tow sack against his left knee, the 44/40 under his right leg in the scabbard. In his shirt pocket he carried a tintype, the one she'd given him. Teddy looked like a strapping boy. Somewhere out there, someone knew something about the lad's whereabouts or his demise. Cal's half squinted eyes studied through the glare of the desert, past the saw tooth mountains he would find the answer about Teddy's fate if he was lucky. His tongue grew thicker with each mile he rode, water never quenched the greater thirst.

Four days later, he still rode through the empty canyons. No wickiups, only a few old fire rings in the cactus-forested hills where he had expected to locate some of them. He found no inhabited *rancherias.*

In late afternoon, he crossed over a range and descended a narrow trail into a chasm. A hint of something teased his nose. When he drew closer, he spotted a grass wickiup under a *palo verde.* At last, he'd found a camp, and the notion gave him new strength.

A bareheaded Apache male came out with a single shot rifle. Cal reined in his horse, his movement slow and non-hostile. He took a hard look at the man and surmised him to be a reservation deserter. The absence of black war paint was one clue. The other was the fact that the rifle was clearly not cocked yet.

"You have come a long ways?" the Apache asked in his own tongue.

"Yes, but I am not the Army or the Indian police."

The man nodded he heard and waved for him to approach. "We once rode together. I know you."

Cal squinted to recall the man's name. A teenage girl came outside and took the reins to his horse.

"My woman will care for it," the Apache said regarding his horse. "My name is Billy Good and I remember yours. It is Jones."

Cal nodded he'd heard the man as he took a small sack from his saddlebags to give to her, before he let her have the reins. When she led the sorrel away he stepped closer to Billy.

"It's been a long time. Why aren't you at San Carlos?" Billy never answered as he indicated to Cal to enter the lodge. He knew when Indians did not wish to speak of something, they ignored the question.

"I gave corn to your wife," he said. His host nodded in gratitude and motioned for him to be seated. Both men took seats on the frayed Navajo blanket spread on the ground. There was no food in sight.

She ducked in with the pouch of flat corn. Without any reaction, she poured it onto her grinding stone and began to crush it as the two men made small talk about old times.

"I came here on a mission," Cal finally said.

Billy nodded. He understood such things.

"Some young broncos took a boy in a raid. A white boy—" He fished out Teddy's picture.

Billy studied the picture, and then he showed it to the woman who nodded, she had seen it too. No clue, Cal knew he was playing poker with tough players—not an eyebrow twitched, not a mouth broke a straight line.

"His mother—she wants her son back. I have come to find him."

"What could you trade for such a boy?" Billy finally asked.

"Whisky. "

Billy nodded his head. "What else?"

"One new Winchester and ammunition," Cal finally said with gut wrenching reluctance. It didn't matter, whisky or guns, both were illegal as hell to trade to known hostiles. If the Army ever learned of such a transaction, he'd be in deep trouble—but the Army had never got Teddy Swain back, either. He looked at the stone face in front of him.

"Whisky, cartridges, rifle. That's all I've got. Can I make a trade with them?"

Billy shrugged. "Most of the broncos are in Mexico."

"Is the boy down there?" Cal demanded.

"Maybe, maybe not. You got whisky and rifle, we go see."

A week later, Cal arrived in Tucson and dismounted heavily. After such a long ride, he was forced to grasp the saddlehorn for several minutes to let his aching legs become sea worthy. Bone weary, he swayed as he crossed her porch to knock on the door. When she opened the door, her eyes flew open in shock. Her face paled when she looked beyond him at the other horse and rider. Finally, she managed a shriek at her discovery.

"You found my boy! Teddy!" She rushed past Cal to hug the quiet boy who slipped from his horse.

"Teddy! Teddy! Are you all right?" she asked, her hands touching his dust-streaked face, searching him for wounds and imperfections.

"I'm fine, Mother." He sounded embarrassed by her attention.

The boy would be better in time. The shock would wear off, Cal felt certain. Teddy Swain had been through a lot, and he'd seen more than most grownups would in a lifetime.

She turned with her eyes filled with tears that she couldn't control. "How can I ever repay you, Mister Jones?"

"Well, ma'am, I reckon fifty bucks would be enough. But I have to warn you that I lost your rifle." He shook his head to silence the boy's protest.

"A rifle? Who cares about a rifle?" She almost laughed aloud at his concern as she wiped at the tears on her cheeks.

"Well, ma'am, let's not talk about it ever again."

"Certainly, Mister Jones. I shall consider the matter settled."

Fine, he didn't figure the boy would mention it, either and perhaps the Army would never learn he had traded a new .44/40 and whisky to some hostile Apaches for the ransom payment. It would just as well be left unsaid.

She paused in the doorway on her way to get his pay and looked back in disbelief at Cal and her son.

"Won't you consider moving in with Teddy and me? We have this large house—"

Cal shook his head. "I learned a lot of things out there." He motioned to the distant mountains. "Lately, I've wondered why I drank so much. Now I know. My scouting days are over. Ain't nothing left for me to do, but three things."

"Oh? What's that?"

"Getting drunk, being drunk, and getting that way again." He waved off her protest. "Don't worry about me, ma'am. You've got a fine boy here to raise. He's plenty tough and he'll make a good man. The Apaches thought so, too."

If they hadn't, the boy wouldn't be alive.

Cal and Teddy shook hands while she went indoors. Neither spoke, but their nods were enough. Then the boy went inside the house.

"Mister Jones!" Colleen rushed back outside. "Here's a hundred dollars, and it's not enough for all you have done. Take that horse, too."

"No ma'am, I have no place to keep him. Besides, I've got no reason to own one."

Unable to contain herself, she took him in a surprise hug and kissed him several times on the cheek. Wet kisses, for she had let the tears run down unheeded since he had arrived with the boy. "You ever need something—anything, money for your whisky, whatever—you come see me."

His face afire with embarrassment, he could only mumble thanks and close his fist on the money she gave him. He stepped back. Then he remembered Gladys. She'd like all the whisky he could afford to buy with this money. Of course, when the word got out he'd brought the boy back, they'd buy him several rounds of drinks in all the bars. But after the notoriety wore off, he'd have to go back to swamping out saloons again.

He looked forward to the whisky that he intended to drink. It would make him forget. Forget growing old. Forget the sad state of his blood brothers, the wild Apache.

His tongue was so thick for need of a drink, he doubted he could even talk as he hurried to find Gladys and share the good news.

DUSTY RICHARDS grew up riding horses and watching his western heroes on the big screen. He even wrote book reports for his classmates, making up westerns since English teachers didn't read that kind of book. His mother didn't want him to be a cowboy, so he went to college, then worked for Tyson Foods and auctioned cattle when he wasn't an anchor on television.

His lifelong dream, though, was to write the novels he loved. He sat on the stoop of Zane Grey's cabin and promised he'd one day get published, as well. In 1992, that promise became a reality when his first book, *Noble's Way,* hit the shelves. In the years since, he's published over 160 more, winning nearly every major award for western literature along the way. His 150th novel, *The Mustanger and the Lady,* was adapted for the silver screen and released as the motion picture *Painted Woman* in 2017. In a review for the movie, *True West* magazine proclaimed Dusty "the greatest living western fiction writer alive."

Sadly, Dusty passed away in early 2018, leaving behind a legion of fans and a legacy of great western writing that will live on for generations.

Facebook: westernauthordustyrichards
www.dustyrichards.com

CPSIA information can be obtained
at www.ICGtesting.com
Printed in the USA
LVHW030851221221
706917LV00003B/327